"Oh Simon, you have no idea how nice it is to feel *welcomed*…

"Why do I feel so at home here?"

Simon had no idea what Penelope meant by that comment, but it pleased him to see her settling in so well.

"I don't know," he replied, "but I'm sure a lot has to do with Sarah."

"Maybe so." She stared at her teacup. "I've also been thinking about what you said earlier—that the sense of emptiness I've always felt might have to do with a lack of faith."

Having never felt that lack, Simon didn't know what to say. "You might consider having a talk with our bishop," he suggested. "He's a *gut* man and might be able to offer some advice."

She looked faintly surprised. "I might do that…"

Simon tried hard not to clutch at a wild hope—that Penelope might someday be baptized Amish so he could court her. It was far too soon in their acquaintance to entertain such thoughts.

But he himself couldn't shake the almost eerie feeling that his future wife was sitting right here in the kitchen with him.

Living on a remote self-sufficient homestead in North Idaho, **Patrice Lewis** is a Christian wife, mother, author, blogger, columnist and speaker. She has practiced and written about rural subjects for almost thirty years. When she isn't writing, Patrice enjoys self-sufficiency projects, such as animal husbandry, small-scale dairy production, gardening, food preservation and canning, and homeschooling. She and her husband have been married since 1990 and have two daughters.

Books by Patrice Lewis

Love Inspired

The Amish Newcomer
Amish Baby Lessons
Her Path to Redemption
The Amish Animal Doctor
The Mysterious Amish Nanny
Their Road to Redemption
The Amish Midwife's Bargain
The Amish Beekeeper's Dilemma
Uncovering Her Amish Past

Visit the Author Profile page at LoveInspired.com.

Uncovering Her Amish Past

PATRICE LEWIS

LOVE INSPIRED
INSPIRATIONAL ROMANCE

LOVE INSPIRED®
INSPIRATIONAL ROMANCE

ISBN-13: 978-1-335-93677-6

Uncovering Her Amish Past

Love Inspired
22 Adelaide St. West, 41st Floor
Toronto, Ontario M5H 4E3, Canada
www.LoveInspired.com

Printed in Lithuania

Recycling programs for this product may not exist in your area.

MIX
Paper | Supporting responsible forestry
FSC® C021394

Fear not: for I have redeemed thee,
I have called thee by thy name; thou art mine.
—*Isaiah* 43:1

To God, for blessing me with my husband and daughters, the best family anyone could hope for.

Chapter One

Penelope Moore peered through the swishing windshield wipers. The tiny town of Pierce, Montana, was no longer visible in her rearview mirror and she was driving on a gravel road through alternating forests of pine trees and broad fields. The summer day was warm, and this rainstorm broke the increasing humidity and offered freshness to the air.

She was on her way to her first assignment of the new job she'd landed two weeks ago as a franchise scout for a company called QuirkyB&B, a bed-and-breakfast franchise. They needed people to research unusual or unique B&Bs around the country and bring them under their corporate umbrella, she was told, and her background in advertising and marketing was especially valuable. They said they were always hiring enthusiastic scouts such as herself.

During her training, Quirky B&B had recommended using an excuse as to why she was booking an extended stay at each location, and Penelope had volunteered that she was an amateur landscape painter. She was told that was the perfect front.

As an added measure of interest, she would be working incognito. Her job was to assess the potential for the

B&B to become a franchise location. The only downside of her training was the unrelenting pressure to convince the independent B&B businesses to franchise.

Even accustomed as she was to the competitive marketing and advertising world, QuirkyB&B's tactics seemed…well, aggressive. However, the rewards were high, with impressive commissions for every new franchisee she brought in.

And Penelope desperately needed the commission she would earn from this assignment.

The only fly in her ointment was her refusal of the corporate requirement that she have a smart phone. Penelope knew she was one of the last urban holdouts against the convenience, but she didn't like the constant connectivity and preferred to keep her communications options simple. The cheap basic flip phone she used didn't permit texts, and her boss didn't push when she dug in her heels on the issue. She promised him she would keep up with emails instead.

So—armed with her simple flip phone and a suitcase full of art supplies—she'd flown from Boston to Montana, rented a car and made her way toward the remote town of Pierce.

This corner of Montana seemed pretty enough. The town wasn't much to see—the sign on the outskirts said the population was 3,500—but she was startled to see one or two Amish buggies on the roads. She had no idea the church had spread this far west, though she'd seen enough of the distinctive sect while growing up in Pennsylvania.

On the long drive, she had thought long and hard how best to approach this undercover assignment. Should she act naive? Haughty? Gossipy? What was the best way to extract the information she needed?

"There it is," she murmured, slowing down. A home-made wooden sign proclaiming Mountain View Bed and Breakfast directed her through an open gate and down a gravel driveway through a tunnel of coniferous trees. Then the foliage opened up and she saw a large and charming two-story board-and-batten home perched on a broad green lawn. The structure had a generous front porch wreathed with Virginia creeper, with homey rocking chairs taking advantage of the view. The house was old, but clearly renovated and well-loved.

Her boss at QuirkyB&B said initial research of the establishment painted a portrait of a business that was amateurish and not well-run, but its location was prime and it had the added novelty of being off the beaten path, which was an attraction to many people. On the downside, apparently it did not have internet service, which would deter some people…unless the lack of internet was itself an attraction for those who needed a break from hyperconnected daily life.

Doubtless, she was told, the owner wouldn't have any problem franchising it. Start-ups were often grateful for a chance to be pulled into a professional organization to expand their marketing…or so her boss assured her. In fact, it was a shoo-in for her first assignment. Easy-peasey.

Penelope parked the car and turned off the engine. In the sudden silence, the rain drumming on the roof was almost deafening. She pressed a hand to her midsection and debated making a run for it through the rain or waiting for the storm cell to pass. She shrugged, got out of the car and dashed for the porch.

She shook her head to dislodge some of the water and wiped the rain from her face. Then she took a deep breath, lifted her chin and knocked on the door.

No answer. The rain pounded on the roof of the porch. She knocked again, louder.

From inside, she heard footsteps approaching and a man opened the door. He had dark curly hair and cheerful blue eyes, and he was dressed in classic Amish attire of broadfall trousers with suspenders over a green shirt. He was only a few inches taller than her, which would put him at a compact five-foot-nine, but wiry. He gave her a casual glance and said, *"Guten tag,* Sarah. *Heute hat es ziemlich geregnet, nicht wahr?"*

Penelope was thrown for a loop, and her greeting died on her lips. She had taken German in high school and had tried to keep up with her studies afterward, but hadn't spoken the language in years. She was able to recognize the greeting as *Hello, Sarah. Quite a rain today, isn't it?* But her brain couldn't work fast enough to formulate a reply.

Suddenly the man did a classic double take and stared at her. "S-Sarah?"

"Good afternoon," she replied. "My name is Penelope Moore. I'll be staying here for the next few weeks as a guest of your B&B."

He snapped shut his open mouth, then peered at her more closely. "Excuse me, I thought you were my sister-in-law Sarah." He scratched his head in a gesture of confusion. "I was wondering what she was doing in *Englisch* clothes."

"Yes. Well." The man seemed positively dazed. "What do I need to do to check in?"

"Please come in. I'm so sorry. You just threw me for a moment." Still appearing confused, the man moved to a small desk area and shuffled around for some paperwork.

She'd had no idea the B&B proprietor was Amish. No wonder it had no internet service. It would also go a long way toward explaining the limited and clumsy on-line presence of the establishment. Certainly he didn't use a computerized check-in process. Everything was done by ledger.

While the man prepared the paperwork, she glanced around at the room, clearly the home's living room that now doubled as a lobby. The hardwood floors gleamed, the simple wooden furniture shone with polish, the upholstered chairs looked comfy, the cream-colored walls were bare of any artwork and wall sconces held a variety of what were unmistakably oil lamps. Along one wall, a well-stocked bookshelf offered a selection of reading material for guests. A set of stairs at one side led to the second floor. It was hard for her to see anything wrong with the lobby. In fact, she appreciated the simple lines and clean furnishings.

"Sign here, please," the man said, interrupting her in-spection and presenting a piece of paper on a clipboard.

Penelope scrawled her signature, then handed over her credit card, which he processed—she was amused to see—using an old-fashioned manual credit-card im-printer. She desperately hoped QuirkyB&B was prompt in reimbursing her expenses, because at the moment she was in far more debt on her credit card than she was comfortable with.

"Danke," he said when she finished. "I mean, thank you."

"Bitte," she replied. "I've had some German when I was younger, though I don't know if I could keep up with a conversation anymore."

He offered her a smile that didn't quite reach his eyes. "I simply can't get over how much you resemble my sister-in-law. Oh, and I should have introduced myself earlier. I'm Simon Troyer. Is this your first time in Montana?"

"Yes. I'm an artist and wanted to stay here for a few weeks to get some painting done."

He didn't blink an eye at her ready-made excuse. "I have your room all ready, but you're the only guest at the moment, so if you need a larger room to set up your art supplies, just let me know. Meanwhile—" he glanced out the front windows "—it looks like the rain has eased. I'll help carry in your luggage. I'm sorry you arrived on a day with such bad weather."

She followed him outside, down the porch steps and toward her vehicle. The sky still dropped a bit of moisture, but the worst of the rain had passed. She handed out two suitcases, then gathered up her fold-up easel and her valise of art supplies. "I'll come back for the canvases later," she said, then glanced around at the dripping trees and grass. "Seems nice out here."

"It is," he agreed. "It's been a wet summer so far, but the rain is always welcome."

"I grew up in Pennsylvania, so I've seen plenty of Amish," she couldn't help but remark. "But I had no idea there was an Amish church in Montana."

The man gave a rusty chuckle. "We're fairly new here. Myself, I've only been here less than a year, and this community has only been around five years or so." He climbed the steps back onto the porch, shouldered open the front door and held it open for her. "Your room is on the second floor."

He climbed the stairs and she followed. The upstairs had a long hallway running the length of the house with numerous closed doors, all beautifully trimmed in golden wood. He opened the nearest door and led the way in.

She almost gasped. The room was lovely. A large window showed a beautiful view of a huge raised-bed garden in the backyard, with pine trees and distant mountains visible. The room was very basic, but clean as a whistle, with cream-colored walls and hardwood floors, bare except for a small rug beside the bed. A bedside table held a lamp. The room had two doors— Simon demonstrated how one was a closet and the other held a small bathroom. The furniture was simple and made from pine—bed, dresser, bedside table and rocking chair. A colorful quilt covered the bed and a vase of flowers sat on the dresser.

"The lamp is battery operated," Simon said, pointing. "This is a Plain establishment, so we're off-grid. I have solar panels, which provide some electricity for the convenience of my guests, and I'm required by law to have refrigeration. However, whenever possible I prefer to use nonelectric options." He set down the suitcases. "If you need internet access, I'm afraid you'll have to go into town."

"I see." Penelope hadn't expected the facility to be quite as primitive as this, but she would make do. "Well, I'm here to paint, not surf the web."

"Also…" Simon hesitated. "Since this is a bed-and-

breakfast—" he emphasized the last word "—I don't advertise that I usually offer an evening meal for a small additional cost. Do you have any food allergies or aversions I should know about?"

"Well, I hate tuna. No allergies."

"Tuna." He nodded. "I'll let you think over the offer. I usually just eat in the kitchen, but there's a small dining room for guests," he added with a bright smile.

"Thank you." Penelope made a mental note of the dinner option, wondering if it was a feature QuirkyB&B would want to know about. "I might take you up on that. It's either that or I have to go into town each evening for a restaurant meal."

"*Ja*, that's why I offered. I find myself doing this regularly for other visitors. Well, I'll let you get settled in. Let me know if you need anything."

"Thank you." She watched as he retreated from the room and closed the door behind him.

She looked around and smiled. According to the QuirkyB&B guidelines she was following, things looked promising. What could possibly go wrong?

Simon descended the stairs toward the lobby, still feeling shocked. The resemblance of his newest guest to his sister-in-law was uncanny. She had the same dark brown eyes of his brother's wife, the same dark hair—which Penelope kept in a long braid down her back—the same slim figure and long neck, even a tiny mole above her eyebrow, though it was not the same eyebrow as Sarah's. And this new woman had signed in using her left hand. Sarah was right-handed.

Aside from that, it was almost like Penelope and

Sarah were twins, something he knew was not the case. Sarah didn't have any siblings—a matter of some sadness to her parents, he remembered. He knew her *mudder und vader* had not been too happy when their only child had decided to immigrate to Montana from Ohio with her *hutband*, looking for better land prices.

He would definitely have to introduce the two women. Imagine finding a stranger that looked just like you! The Germans had a word for it: *doppelgänger*.

Meanwhile, he had work to do. He had managed to get the upstairs and lobby areas of this building finished in time to open for business, but his personal living quarters and the kitchen still needed work. He had a lot to do…and a lot to prove.

He resumed what he had been doing before his newest guest's arrival, glazing a windowpane for a refurbished back door.

His private quarters were, frankly, a mess. None of the perfection from the front of the house carried through to the back, where he maintained his bedroom, a small parlor space and a private back porch leading out into the vast raised-bed garden area where he grew much of what he served at mealtimes.

Here, the walls were bare studs—he had only just finished installing insulation—and tools were scattered everywhere. Simon picked his way amid the chaos and reached for the window-glazing putty. He frowned as he continued his task, thinking over the last year or so, praying his business would succeed.

When he'd come across this battered old farmhouse on three acres just outside the boundaries of the Amish settlement, he knew it was meant for him. Against his father's wishes, he'd bought the property and started the long road toward fixing up the building.

Now he was in a position to accept guests. He had focused on the cosmetic areas visitors were likely to see first, but he was nowhere near finished with the renovations.

As he worked, his mind felt unsettled. All his life, he had felt the weight of his father's disapproval over his choices. If this business venture failed, he would be forced to crawl home, humiliated that his *daed* had been proved right...

"Excuse me?"

"Ja?" Startled, he jerked his head up from his work. Penelope stood in the doorway of his private quarters, eyeing the chaos of the room with what seemed like distaste. He stood up, a pot of glazing in one hand and a putty knife in the other, and felt both irritated and embarrassed at the intrusion into his private rooms, especially in such a state of disarray.

"I wonder if I could look through your gardens behind the house?" She gestured.

"Ja sure." The words came automatically. He'd given tours of his garden in the past, and felt it couldn't hurt to show this long-term guest around. After all, she was helping to contribute to the financial success of his establishment. "Would you like a tour?"

She inclined her head. "Thank you."

She was certainly as pretty as his sister-in-law, he decided, but Sarah would never act so standoffish. Simon laid aside his tools and brushed off his hands. "If you'll excuse the mess, you're welcome to come through this back door." It wasn't as if she could unsee the construction debris at this stage anyway. "As you may have noticed, I refurbished the front of the house first so I could make it ready for visitors, but I'm still working back here."

"I can see that." She sidestepped around a sawhorse and nodded as he held the door open for her. "Most hotel rooms are so bland and uniform, so this B&B is certainly…different."

He stiffened at the implied criticism. "Do you travel a lot?" he inquired, keeping his tone pleasant. He snatched his hat and plopped it on his head.

She hesitated a moment. "More and more," she said. "Since I'm an artist, I tend to go where the painting takes me."

"I have no artistic talent," he remarked, striding toward the tall deer netting that protected the vegetable garden. "I admire those who do."

"This is nice," she admitted, stepping through the garden gate he held open for her.

"Danke." Simon smiled. It might be *hochmut*, but he was proud of his garden.

The verdant area—still wet from the rain—consisted entirely of tidy rectangular raised beds. In several locations, archways connected two beds, under which he could walk to pick beans or peas or other climbing vegetables. Fruit trees grew along the edges. From this space, he harvested almost everything he needed to create the meals he served. In fact, he was trying to make it a selling point to serve foods grown or raised within the church settlement.

"And you have chickens!" Penelope gravitated toward a huge enclosed yard where a rooster kept an eye on his flock.

"Almost everything I serve at meals comes from here," he said, gesturing to take in both the chickens and the garden beds. "I purchase meats from other church members, so everything is organic and raised within just a mile or two."

She raised a single eyebrow in a manner remarkably like his sister-in-law. "I see." She looked around. "Would you object if I were to set up my easel and do some paintings out here?"

"*Nein*, of course not. Where do you sell your paintings?"

He didn't expect her to look cornered, but suddenly she did. Somehow he assumed that if she could afford to spend several weeks at his B&B, then her art must be very successful. But she seemed shocked at the question.

"Oh, h-here and there," she stuttered, and waved vaguely with her hand. "I've… I've built up a clientele who enjoy my work."

"I see." He didn't see, but could think of no other response. He knew nothing about the art world or how it worked. For all he knew, she had a patron who supported her lifestyle. It was none of his business, as long as she paid her way at his establishment.

He walked her around the garden, pointing out its features. "If you have a favorite vegetable," he ventured, "I can let you know if it's ready to harvest and prepare it for tonight's dinner." He pointed at some beds of broccoli, where the crowns looked full and inviting.

"Do you grow tuna?" she asked, a gleam of humor in her eyes.

Simon laughed outright. He had a feeling Penelope would be a *gut* guest. He liked her sense of humor.

Chapter Two

Tuna. Back in her room, Penelope grimaced at her wise-crack. What had inspired her to come up with that bit of nonsense? At least Simon had laughed. She liked his laugh. It was unaffected and hearty, and somehow contagious.

In fact, she was impressed with his impeccable hospitality. She could find no fault with either his demeanor or with the establishment's facilities. She could recognize how much work he had done on the older building to make it shine—just glimpsing the chaos still going on in his private quarters was proof of that—and his garden was nothing short of stunning.

In fact, the garden was hugely attractive to her. Looking out her bedroom window from the second floor, she could better see the precise layout and appreciate how lush and beautiful it was.

She had gardened with her parents when she was younger, but the last few years of urban life made her realize how much she missed getting her hands dirty. She knew it wasn't in her job description as a scout to offer to help weed or water the vegetables, but it was tempting.

She just hoped she could keep up the facade of working incognito. *Think of the money*, she told herself through gritted teeth. Her last credit card bill was simply a reminder that she was on the right course of action to get out of debt.

She sighed and turned to unzip the suitcase holding her art supplies. This part of the deception was at least truthful. Penelope hadn't sold any paintings, but she had given away a lot. Most of her work was done for sheer enjoyment. She loved painting. She often just itched to paint. Her work wasn't the best in the world—she was her own worst critic—but that didn't prevent her from enjoying the process.

The fact that she had somehow landed right on the edge of an Amish settlement filled her with interest. She could, in her mind's eye, visualize endless paintings based on traditional Amish themes: colorful quilts hanging from lines, rays of sunshine streaming into a room of Plain furniture, a horse-drawn buggy trotting down a gravel road, with a trail of dust in its wake... Yes, the possibilities for artistic expression were endless.

As for Simon—well, Penelope found herself disliking the thought of deceiving him in any way. It was always that way with the Amish people she knew growing up. Their godly lifestyle and honest outlook made her feel like she should be on her best behavior. She felt ashamed to deceive Simon about her reasons for being here.

Penelope dropped down in the rocking chair and stared out the window. The familiar nagging sense of something missing tickled at her. She'd had that feeling for as long as she could remember, and she couldn't imagine why. Certainly it didn't stem from her upbringing, which had been filled with love and support from her parents. Nor did it stem from a lack of friends or even of meaningful work. It was just…there. Hovering in the background, quietly tugging at her heart.

Mostly she could ignore it, but once in a while it flared up for some reason, and she wondered why she felt it now.

The sense of longing was coupled with another dull realization, that she didn't have a sense of home. She felt no particular attachment to the town where she grew up, aside from a natural desire to see friends and family. Nor did she feel called to remain in any other location. She sometimes felt like a lost soul, wondering if she'd ever find where she belonged.

Well, it was a lifelong question that she had yet to answer. Unwilling to examine the sensation further, Penelope rose and began unfolding her portable easel. After a moment's debate, she set it up in a corner of the room, out of the direct sun—or what she assumed would be direct sun when the clouds parted—but which received plenty of natural light. She spread a cloth on top of the bureau to protect the wood, then laid out her acrylic paints. The canvases were still in her car, so she contented herself for the moment on making a series of drawings in a sketchbook, starting with the view from her bedroom of the garden outside.

Immersed as she was, she didn't realize how much time had passed until she heard a knock at the door. "Miss Moore? Dinner is ready."

"Thank you!" she called. She laid down her sketchbook, patted down her hair and tugged her blouse neat, and left her bedroom.

Simon had laid out a single place setting in a small

dining room off the kitchen she hadn't noticed before. The room had several tables to accommodate more guests, and he had placed her near a window with a view toward the chicken coop. A large service window allowed guests to see the activity in the kitchen and permitted Simon to keep an eye on the diners.

Whatever he was cooking smelled divine. "Chicken potpie," he answered in reply to her inquiry. "A lady from our church raises chickens, my next-door neighbor grew the wheat for the flour in the pie crust, I buy milk and butter from another church member, and all the vegetables and herbs came from the garden out back. The only commercial ingredient is Worcestershire sauce."

"Wow." To her, that was a truly monumental accomplishment. She sat down and he served the meal with subtle attention.

But eating alone seemed unusual, especially when she noticed him standing in the kitchen, eating his own dinner, just as he mentioned earlier. Impulsively she called, "No need to eat in the kitchen, if you'd like to join me."

He seemed surprised at the invitation, and hesitated. Then he shrugged, picked up his plate and emerged into the dining room.

"Thank you," he said, sitting down opposite.

In the interest of deepening her knowledge of his establishment—and to satisfy her own curiosity about the man, she said, "Tell me about this B&B. How long have you been in business?"

"Just a couple of months. I'm only getting started."

"What inspired you to open it?"

He eyed her with what seemed like suspicion. "Aptitude."

"Aptitude? You mean you have a knack for hospitality?"

"*Ja*. Most people have been pleased with their stay here."

A good detail for her report to QuirkyB&B, she thought. "I've stayed in a few B&Bs before, and usually it's the women who do the cooking. It's rather unusual to see a man, especially an Amish man, in the kitchen."

He shrugged with, she thought, a touch of defensiveness. "So my *daed* always said. I brought my youngest sister out here last year and she thought about staying on to focus on the kitchen duties, but she got a better-paying offer back home and so she went back. But my *graemmaemm* taught me to cook, especially when she learned I wanted to operate a B&B. She said it was a skill I should know. Since I'm not married, she's right. I've had a few chefs show me some of their tricks and I've done a lot of experimenting."

She touched her half-empty plate with the fork. "It shows. If this is any example, you've learned well. I enjoy cooking, too. I won't call myself a gourmet cook, but I find it fun and relaxing to putter in the kitchen."

Abruptly he changed the subject. "If you're interested in seeing a bit of the Amish community, I'd like to walk you over to my brother's farm and introduce you to my sister-in-law. As I said, you bear a striking resemblance to her. It might be interesting for you two to meet."

She raised her eyebrows. "Are we that similar?"

"*Ja*. If you've heard the term *doppelgänger*, you'll know what I mean. Two strangers who happen to look alike."

She gave him a half smile. "Then yes, I think it would

be interesting to meet her. If I'm going to be painting some scenes here during my stay, then seeing more of the community is useful." She took a bite of the pie.

"Besides—" he forked up the last of his meal "—I think you'll like Sarah, and since you'll be lodging here for a few weeks, it might be nice for you to have a friend. I imagine it's a lonely existence for you, being on the road so much with your art."

Penelope blinked back sudden moisture. How observant of this stranger. His words tied in to that nagging feeling of something missing in her life and she wondered if that was a clue as to why.

It was true she had very few friends, and wasn't into the nightlife scene as so many of her coworkers were, a subject of much ribbing back in the office. The truth was, she didn't feel at ease with her colleagues and preferred the solitude of painting over noisy venues.

"I'm a bit of an introvert," she summarized. Her tone was a bit more defensive than she anticipated. "I relate better to my canvases than I do to other people."

He chuckled. "I'm much the same way," he admitted. "The hours I spend working in the garden alone are some of my favorite times."

She grew curious. "This community is so far off the beaten track—don't you ever get lonely?"

"Nein," he replied simply, as if the question surprised him. "I have my church community. What more do I need?"

Penelope had attended church a few times growing up—her parents had taken a casual approach to faith—so she had never been involved in a church. And while she understood at some level that the Amish withdrew from modern society to focus on their beliefs, she had always vaguely assumed it was more hardship than comfort.

Yet Simon seemed to imply the opposite. Interesting.

He rose from his seat and picked up his empty plate. "I have some apple goodie for dessert, if you'd like a sweet."

"Apple goodie? What's that?" She forked up the remainder of her meal and set the cutlery on the plate.

"It's a baked-apple dish with crispy crumbles on top. Very popular among tourists. I think you'll like it." He picked up both his and her plates and left the dining room.

She eyed him as he went about his task in the kitchen. His curly hair had a bit of an impression from his straw hat. His movements were clean and efficient. His appearance was very different than that of her urban co-workers, and to her surprise she found she liked the air of earthiness about him.

Most distinctive, however, was the expression of peace on his face. No, not just his face. Somehow, he gave off an air of tranquility that seemed more than skin-deep. Her impression was the quality was ingrained and was the source of handling any day-to-day challenges from guests with composure.

Somehow she doubted Simon ever experienced that nagging sense of something missing.

"There you go," he said, placing the apple dessert in front of her. "Take your time, and you can just leave the plate on the table when you're finished. Would you be troubled if I slipped out to go talk with my brother and sister-in-law? It would mean you'd be alone in the house."

"No, that's fine." *I could snoop*, she thought, and immediately dismissed the thought. That was too underhanded, no matter how much information she might gather. "It's been a long day anyway, so I'll just go to my room."

"*Danke*. I want to ask my sister-in-law if tomorrow is a convenient time to visit. They don't live too far away and I won't be gone long."

He walked through the parlor, plucked his hat off a hook and left the house. It was very quiet after he left. His absence made her realize how much quiet presence he carried with him.

Simon walked through the sunset toward his brother's farm. He couldn't explain why he felt such a sense of urgency to have his new guest meet his sister-in-law other than he couldn't get over their physical similarities… although, if he was truthful with himself, he thought Penelope's personality was more vibrant and interesting than Sarah's.

His brother Amos lived less than a mile away. Simon knew the family would be gathered in the living room after their evening meal. Their two small children would be playing on the floor, Amos would be reading *The Budget* and Sarah would doubtless be knitting. He sometimes envied the domestic tranquility of his brother's family and hoped one day he, too, could find a woman to court so he could experience similar happiness. Maybe someone like Penelope…except Amish, of course.

Sure enough, after he knocked and was invited indoors, he found his relatives in just the positions he anticipated, except Sarah was rocking her eighteen-month-old daughter, Eleanor, rather than knitting. His three-year-old nephew, Paul, squealed. "Uncle Simon!"

"*Gut'n owed*, niblet." He picked up the boy and swung him around, then gave him an exaggerated smack on the cheek.

"It's late for a visit," remarked Amos, putting aside his newspaper.

"*Ja*, well, I have an unusual request." Simon put the boy back down on the floor. He addressed Sarah. "I have a new guest who checked in today. She's an artist and plans to spend several weeks at the B&B. I think you should meet her."

"Why is that?" His sister-in-law eyed him with curiosity.

"Because she looks just like you. And I mean *just* like you. It's…it's uncanny."

Sarah's eyebrows rose. "How unusual."

"More than you know. When she first checked in, I honestly thought she *was* you and I wondered why you were wearing *Englisch* clothes. At any rate, I wondered if you minded if I brought her around sometime tomorrow."

"*Ja*, of course." Sarah smiled, her dark eyes crinkling. "Now I'm curious to meet her. Bring her by. We can have tea."

"Now I'm curious, too." Amos smiled. "I'm the most blessed man in the world to have one of my Sarah. I can't imagine there's anyone else like her."

"Well, I think you might be surprised," said Simon. "I'm thinking she's your *doppelgänger.*"

"The children usually nap midmorning," Sarah replied. "Ask if she can come by around eleven o'clock tomorrow morning and we won't be as interrupted."

"I'll do that. *Sayn dich.*" Simon smiled at his relatives, touched little Paul on the head and left the house.

The evening air smelled sweet as he walked back to his house. The sun had set and the shadows under the pine trees were thick. Simon breathed deep of the cooling air. He heard the whine of nightjars diving after insects and a distant yip of a coyote, and saw the dark shapes of white-tailed deer browsing on buds. Even though his father hadn't approved of his moving to Montana, Simon liked it here. A lot.

The dining room was empty when he entered the house. He hesitated a moment, wondering if he should go upstairs to inform Penelope of his sister-in-law's invitation, when a movement outside caught his eye.

She was walking among the border of flowers he had planted outside the garden fence. He paused in the darkened room, knowing he couldn't be seen, and watched.

Yes, she was startlingly similar to his sister-in-law, even in her *Englisch* clothes. Yet Sarah had a certain quiet confidence about her that seemed to be lacking in Penelope. It made sense; Sarah was among her own people, while this new guest was not.

She paused to sniff a rose. Her neck was slender and graceful, and the male in him couldn't help but admire her appearance. He had never entertained unbrotherly thoughts about Sarah, and in his mind it seemed odd to admire someone who looked like her.

But Sarah was sedate and calm. Penelope seemed to have higher spirits and a more vibrant personality, despite her claim to be an introvert. Maybe it was the introvert in him that responded to that quality. Whatever the chemistry, he liked being around her.

He went outside. "Good evening."

"Good evening." She straightened. "It seemed too nice an evening to stay cooped up indoors."

"*Ja*, I agree. Don't hesitate to take advantage of the rocking chairs on the front porch. I just got back from my brother's house," he added. "My sister-in-law Sarah is interested in meeting you. She said the children will be napping around eleven o'clock tomorrow morning, if that's a convenient time for you."

"Of course. How many children does she have?"

"Two. Little Paul is three years old, and they have an eighteen-month-old daughter, Eleanor."

To his surprise, she gave a little sigh. "It must be nice."

"What must be nice?" he asked. "Having children?"

"Yes. It's sometimes hard for career women to think about a family, but I'm of the age where it's more on my mind."

"But surely being an artist isn't incompatible with having a family?" he asked, puzzled. "After all, your hours are your own, aren't they?"

"Oh. Um, yes, you're right. My hours are my own." In the growing darkness of evening, it seemed she had almost a panicked look on her face. As pretty as she was, he wondered why she wasn't married.

He shrugged. It was none of his business. "I'm going to go finish tidying the kitchen," he told her. "Will breakfast at eight o'clock suit, or do you have a different time you prefer?"

"Eight o'clock is fine. I can get a little work done before visiting your relatives. Oh, that reminds me, I need to get the canvases from my car."

"May I help?"

"Yes, please. They're bulky things."

He followed her to the vehicle, where she opened the back door and withdrew a number of art boards of various sizes. "I'll take the larger ones if you want to take the smaller," he offered.

"Thank you." She gathered up the dozen or so medium pieces, while he made a stack of the larger canvases and hefted them in his arms.

She led the way indoors and he followed her up the stairs carrying his bulky burden. She bumped open the door with her hip and tumbled the canvases on the bed.

"Where shall I put these?" he asked, his voice muffled behind the art sheets.

"Hang on, I'll take them." One by one she off-loaded the pieces and stacked them against the wall. "I picked these up just after I got the rental car since I wasn't sure when I'd be near an art store again."

"I see." Curious, he glanced around the room. She had set up an easel in one corner and spread types of paint on a sheet across the dresser. A glass jar held a dozen brushes of various sizes. "I've never seen anyone paint before."

"Does no one paint in town?" she asked, surprised.

"Among the *Englisch* in Pierce? I'm sure they do," he replied. "But here in the church community, it's…well, not exactly discouraged, but neither is it encouraged. Such skill leads to pride—*hochmut*—and it spotlights the individual. We prefer to emphasize community."

"I see." Her eyebrows drew together in a manner similar to his sister-in-law's.

He could tell she didn't understand or approve of the sentiment. "We do have one woman who's clever with drawing," he remarked. "I guess you could say she's an artist of sorts. But she doesn't draw to show anything off. She's just *gut* at it."

"Hmm. Maybe I should meet *her*, too." The words were sharp, but somehow he caught a bit of mischief behind them. Meeting her eyes, he saw a glint of humor.

It was the second time he'd seen her in that kind of mood, and was amazed what it did to her. She looked... well, cute.

He offered a smile. "If you'll be here for any length of time, I'm sure you will. I'm also sure you'll be interested in exploring both the town and our church settlement."

"What do you mean by 'settlement'?" she asked in a puzzled tone.

"*Ja*, I guess you wouldn't know. It's this valley to the east of town..." He gestured in the general direction. "A few years ago, a huge ranch came up for sale. No one was buying it because it was so big and remote, but relatively speaking the price was right for the amount of land. The church bought it and invited people who had been crowded out of more expensive farms east of the Mississippi to settle out here. We're not a town, just a collection of farms within the boundary of the old ranch. The people buying up land are something of a mishmash from all different states and such, but it's an opportunity many of us didn't have in more crowded areas."

"No kidding." She sounded interested. "And how many church members have moved here so far?"

"Maybe twenty-five families or so, which means about 125 people, give or take. Because we hold our church services in homes, rather than using a dedicated building, we may have to split into two districts as we get more people. There will come a point where we can't all fit into any one person's home or barn."

"And this house?" Penelope gestured around the room. "You came from Ohio, then renovated it to open a B&B?"

"*Ja*. My father..." He hesitated. "Never mind." He was about to confess his father's disapproval over his career choice, but decided against it. Instead he said, "I'm going to shut the house down for the night. *Gude nacht.*"

"*Gude nacht,*" she replied with the slight twinkle in her eyes, as if she was pleased to speak the German words.

He made his way downstairs. He had to admit, Penelope was certainly every bit as pretty as his sister-in-law, yet he could already detect differences in their personalities. It's not like they were twins, after all. Still, he wondered how the two women would react when they met.

Chapter Three

Penelope woke up just as the sun peeked over the horizon, and stretched luxuriantly in bed. She looked around at the room, taking pleasure in its clean lines. The wood floors and furniture glowed golden in the early-morning light. She had slept with the window open to take advantage of the sweet fresh air. Yesterday's clouds were gone, and it promised to be a lovely day.

It was a far cry from her apartment in Boston, where the never-ending sounds of traffic made opening her fourth-story window at night less than restful. As she listened to the birdsong, she decided she liked it here.

Last night after Simon left her room, she had duly written down the brief history of the community and what he'd said about how he'd come to purchase this house. Would he be interested in franchising with QuirkyB&B? That was what she was here to convince him to do, after all, but now she had her doubts. He seemed too independent and determined to succeed on his own terms to be interested in coming under a corporate umbrella. The easy conquest implied by her boss may not be so easy after all, despite the advantages of the professional marketing services QuirkyB&B could offer to Simon's start-up business.

If she couldn't convince him…well, she didn't know how that would affect her standing with her employer, but she certainly knew how it would affect her financially. No franchise, no commission.

Still, it was only her first full day here. She had time to work on it. Meanwhile, she could look forward to getting some painting done, and today she was going to meet this mystery woman Simon claimed looked just like her.

She dressed. It was a bit early for breakfast, but she heard a clink or two coming from downstairs and hoped she could get a cup of tea.

When she descended the stairs and entered the dining room, the delectable smells of bacon and sausages came to her. Through the service window of the kitchen, she could see Simon working. He hadn't noticed her. His dark curly hair caught a shaft of early sunlight, which gave it the faintest auburn tinge. His eyes were lowered, intent on some task. He was a handsome man, she decided. She wondered why he wasn't married.

"Guder mariye," she greeted him.

His head snapped up and he gave her a professional smile. *"Guder mariye.* I'm sorry, breakfast isn't ready yet."

"I was just hoping I could get a cup of tea?"

"Ja, of course. Give me a moment…" He went to the sink to wash his hands.

Peering over the ledge of the service window, she saw he had been engaged in rolling out biscuits.

He snatched a towel to dry his hands. "You said tea, not coffee, *ja?"*

"Yes, please. I don't care for coffee."

He chuckled. "Just like Sarah. I usually set things up in the dining area," he added, "but since you're the only guest, you're welcome to come into the kitchen and let me know which kind of tea you prefer."

Penelope went into the kitchen. It was an opportunity to note his standard of culinary cleanliness for her report to QuirkyB&B. The room was clearly a farmhouse kitchen, not a commercial kitchen, but except for the expected disorder associated with preparing a meal, it was scrupulously clean. She was delighted to note a wood cookstove in one corner, though it was not in use at the moment. She noticed the kitchen had no microwave and no small appliances.

From a cabinet, Simon pulled a basket filled with assorted tea bags and set it on the opposite side of the large worktable where he had been rolling out the biscuits. He bustled about heating up water and providing milk and sugar. He withdrew a generous-sized ceramic mug and indicated she was welcome to sit, then placed the mug on the table. "Do you mind if I continue working?"

"Of course not."

"*Danke.* The batch of biscuits in the oven is nearly done. I'm making extra to bring with us when we go visiting. Sarah says my biscuits are even better than hers." He gave her a cheeky smile, peeked into the oven, then continued cutting biscuits.

"So how old is your sister-in-law?" she asked.

"She's twenty-eight."

"Same age as me. And she already has two children?"

"*Ja,* she and my brother have been married six years now."

"So she married young."

"Not really." He looked surprised. "That's about the average age Amish women get married."

"How old is your brother?"

"Thirty. Two years older than me."

"So we're the same age, you and I?"

"Apparently, *ja*."

"I see." She watched as he folded the dough, rolled it, then cut biscuits with efficient movements. "On a different note, if you're Amish, you don't have a telephone, do you? How do customers make reservations?"

"I do have a phone. I just try not to use it." He gave her that cheeky smile again. "But sometimes it's unavoidable in a business, even an Amish one. But most of my reservations come by email, just like yours did."

"Your website is fairly basic."

"Well, it works, doesn't it? I figure my focus should be on the food and hospitality when people arrive, not on computer stuff."

"But you realize, of course, the website is what will connect you to your customers in the first place?"

He scowled. "I don't know how to use computers well. An *Englisch* friend designed the website, and I think it's fine."

She decided not to push, and changed the subject. "I think, after breakfast, I'll do some sketches of your garden, if you don't mind."

"Of course not. I figure we'll walk over to my brother's around ten thirty. It's not quite a mile away."

"Don't you want to drive?" The moment the words were out of her mouth, she slapped a hand to her forehead. "Sorry, I mean in my car."

"It's a nice day for a walk anyway." He grinned at her discomfiture. "People from the church community often walk this road on the way to town, so we'll probably pass a few." He chuckled. "It wouldn't surprise me if they reacted the same way I did when I first saw you, mistaking you for Sarah."

While Penelope was mildly curious to meet the man's sister-in-law, most of her willingness to go was to meet some other Amish members of the community. It had been years since she'd been around the church group, and then only in passing during her childhood in Pennsylvania.

She watched as he cracked eggs into a bowl, then snipped fresh chives and a small amount of rosemary and beat the eggs with the herbs. He removed the bacon from its pan to drain, then poured the eggs into the same pan.

Within minutes, a full breakfast was before her, complete with homemade butter and jam for the biscuits.

"This is incredible," she mumbled with her mouth full. She couldn't remember having such delicious food in years. "You're an amazing cook. You're going to make some lucky woman very happy one day." To her surprise, she felt a flash of wistfulness. It was too easy to see herself in that lucky woman's place.

"Danke." He crunched on a piece of bacon. "That's what Sarah often tells me. I enjoy cooking."

He continued baking as she finished eating, then he lined a basket with a clean cloth and started packing in the biscuits as they cooled.

He glanced at a clock as she finished up. "You'll have about two hours before we leave, if you wanted to do some work in the garden. *Nein*, leave the dishes, I'll take care of them. I'll let you know when it's time to leave."

Penelope nodded her thanks and went upstairs to fetch her sketchbook. The two hours she spent in the garden passed rapidly as she became absorbed in drawing flowers, a trellis with climbing beans, the chickens clucking in their yard and other pastoral scenes.

As she sketched, she came to admire the extensive garden more and more. A serious amount of work had gone into creating and maintaining these extensive growing beds. Could QuirkyB&B really offer any improvement on what Simon was offering his customers? From what she'd seen so far, the only area where he could use some improvement was his online presence, and that was easily remedied...

"Ready?" called Simon from the back door of the house.

"Yes." Penelope straightened up. She wasn't sure she liked the directions her thoughts were going. Would her job be jeopardized if she was to recommend this business *not* be brought under the QuirkyB&B umbrella? She doubted it, but it would certainly mean forfeiting the commission she was depending on so much. She welcomed the distraction of meeting Simon's sister-in-law.

She dropped her sketchbook on a table in the parlor and fell into step beside him as he strode down the gravel road.

"What is it your brother and sister-in-law do?" she inquired, trying to make conversation.

"My brother is a farmer. My sister-in-law splits her time between the farm and the children," Simon explained. "I'm fairly certain Amos—that's my brother—

will be at the house when we arrive. I think he's curious to see you, too."

She felt a trace of annoyance. "I wonder if I should feel like an animal in a zoo. Is *everyone* going to want to see me?"

"*Ja* sure," he replied, as if it were obvious. "Everyone knows Sarah, of course, so everyone will assume you're her. At least at first. Meanwhile, let me tell you about what we're passing…"

He pointed out birds, trees, flowers and crops as they walked along the road. The artist in her realized the remarkable scope of possibilities for painting some beautiful pictures in this part of the world.

"Ah, there's my brother's house," said Simon. He gestured.

Penelope looked ahead and saw a pretty clapboard home with Virginia creeper growing along the porch rails. Did this Sarah truly look like her? She would find out soon enough.

A woman in a blue dress and black apron moved around the porch, watering some plants. As Penelope and Simon approached, he raised his voice. "*Guten tag*, Sarah."

Sarah raised her head, and Penelope gasped and stopped in her tracks. She felt the blood drain from her face. She might as well have been looking at a mirror.

Simon heard Penelope draw in her breath, and he glanced over and saw she had gone as white as a sheet. She had a hand against her throat. Was she going to faint?

He glanced at Sarah. His sister-in-law also stood frozen, staring. There was a moment's silence, punctuated only by birdsong.

"Komm," he urged gently. *"Komm* and meet Sarah." He started walking toward the house, and Penelope stumbled after him.

Sarah descended the porch steps and walked toward them, looking stunned. As the two women grew close, Simon performed the introduction. "Sarah, this is my guest, Penelope Moore. Penelope, this is Sarah Troyer."

It was like the women didn't even hear him. They stared at each other, expressions of utter shock on their faces. Close together, their resemblance, as he suspected, was uncanny.

Long moments passed. After a minute's tense silence, Sarah reached out a hand that trembled slightly and touched Penelope at the corner of her right eyebrow, where a tiny mole enhanced the luminosity of her eyes. "I have one too," she murmured, withdrawing her hand and touching her left eyebrow.

Penelope closed her gaping mouth. "M-mother always told me that's where an angel kissed me," she stuttered. "Sarah…are you thinking what I'm thinking?"

Simon saw Sarah's eyes grow moist. "It's the only explanation I can think of…"

"C-could we be twins?"

"M-maybe," Sarah replied in a shaking voice. She pressed a hand to her forehead. "I can't believe this…"

Simon glanced over as his brother Amos walked toward the group. When he saw Penelope, his jaw dropped.

"Penelope, this is my brother Amos," said Simon.

She dragged her gaze away from Sarah and nodded at

Amos. "Nice to meet you. I'm sorry, I feel shell-shocked. This is incredible…"

"W-when is your birthday?" stammered Sarah.

"January 16," replied Penelope. "I'm twenty-eight."

His sister-in-law closed her eyes and swayed slightly. Amos grabbed her in his arms. "We must be twins," she whispered. "I have the same birthday."

"I'm adopted," said Penelope. "But my parents never told me I had a twin."

"I'm also adopted." Sarah straightened up. "My parents couldn't have children. But *ja*, I never knew I had a twin."

"I wonder if either of your parents even knew?" mused Simon.

"You mean, an adoption agency that split up twins on purpose?" asked Amos. "That's highly unethical."

"But not unheard of." Simon rubbed his chin.

"I'm going to have to talk to my parents and see what they know." Penelope gave a tremulous smile. "In the meantime…" She held open her arms, and Sarah pitched into them. The women hugged long and hard. Both started crying.

Simon felt his throat close up. What an incredible reunion to witness.

After a few moments, both women drew back and sniffed. "*Komm* inside," invited Sarah. "We have a lot to talk about."

Simon followed as the group mounted the porch steps and went indoors. Sarah gestured toward the chairs around the kitchen table, where tea things were already set out. A kettle on the stove steamed silently.

"I want to hear everything," said Penelope, sinking

into a chair. "You said you were adopted, but you don't know who your birth parents were?"

"Nein." Sarah poured water into all the mugs around the table, then set the kettle back on the stove. She took a seat opposite Penelope. "All I was told is that an Amish girl—a *youngie*—got herself in trouble and then ran away from home. She gave her baby to an adoption agency, which reached out to our church because the girl requested the baby be placed with an Amish family. My parents couldn't have children, so they took me. As far as I know, my birth mother disappeared. No one knows what happened to her."

"But if your—our—birth mother had twins, why would the agency split us up? That makes no sense."

"I don't know if either of us could answer that. We're going to have to ask our parents."

Penelope stared at her mug with the steeping tea bag. "I think I remember my mother saying the adoption agency had gone out of business when I was a teenager, but it wasn't an issue that was important to me so I didn't pay much attention."

"H-how was your childhood?" inquired Sarah hesitantly. "Was it happy?"

"Yes, extremely." Penelope smiled. "Like you, I was an only child, and my parents are wonderful. Very supportive, very loving."

"Ja, that's *gut*. So are mine." Sarah's eyes crinkled. "Won't they be surprised when they hear the news!"

Simon watched the dawning friendship between the two women, and his heart swelled.

"Simon says you're an artist?" inquired Sarah.

"Yes." Simon saw Penelope hesitate. "I specialize in

landscapes and scenery. I like to travel to see new vistas. I honestly had no idea there was an Amish settlement here, though since I grew up in Pennsylvania, I saw a lot of church members around." She gave a tentative smile. "I just never knew I was born in the church."

"What church do you go to now?" asked Sarah.

The smile was wiped from Penelope's face. "I don't. My parents weren't especially religious."

"I see." Simon could tell Sarah was holding back any hint of pity at her sister's lack of faith, but he could see the compassion in her eyes. Instead she said, "You should attend one of our church services sometime. Won't people be surprised!"

Penelope chuckled. "Yes, I guess they would. Oh, Sarah... I hardly can believe this. All my life I felt a nagging feeling like something was missing. I wonder if that something was you? Have you had that same feeling?"

"*Nein*, I haven't. Yet..." Sarah smiled. "Yet now that I meet you, I feel more...complete? Is that the right word?"

Just then Simon heard his little niece start to cry from one of the bedrooms. Amos stood up. "The *boppli* is awake. I'll get her." He left the table.

"And I should get home." Simon stood up and looked at Penelope. "Do you want to stay and visit further? You know the way back to the B&B."

"Let me stay just long enough to meet my niece, then I'll go with you. I have a lot to process." She looked at Sarah. "I hope we can get together a lot while I'm here."

"*Ja* sure, of course!" Sarah smiled with enthusiasm. "I wouldn't have it any other way!"

Amos returned with a sleepy toddler in his arms. With

a soft clucking noise, Sarah took the child in her arms. The girl snuggled up against her mother, still drowsy.

"She's lovely," said Penelope softly. Simon glanced at his guest and saw a look of stark longing on her face as she gazed at the child. "I hope I can come back later and meet your son."

"Now that you know the way, come over anytime," invited Amos. "You're always welcome."

"Thank you." Penelope rose to her feet, and Simon saw a sparkle of moisture in her eyes. "A sister," she murmured. "I have a sister."

"And so do I." Sarah smiled up at her. "*Gott* be with you, Penelope."

Simon watched the unfolding relationship between his guest and his sister-in-law. How often did anyone get to witness a reunion between separated twins? Simon found he enjoyed Penelope's company…and watching her with Sarah was something marvelous.

Chapter Four

~≈~

A few minutes later, Penelope walked down the road with Simon at her side.

"Knowing my brother and his wife as well as I do," he observed, "I know their invitation is serious. Don't hesitate to visit. It seems you and Sarah have a lot to learn about each other."

"I feel shocked." Penelope gazed out at the woodsy area they were passing through. "An identical twin sister. I had no idea."

"This is one of those times I wish the Amish used telephones," he said. "I'm sure Sarah is burning with curiosity to grill her parents about the circumstances of her adoption, but they're all the way back in Pennsylvania. I suspect she'll be writing them a letter today, but it will take at least a week to get a response."

"Well, I intend to call my parents right away," replied Penelope. "I want some answers, though I don't know if they'll have any. They've always been very up-front about telling me I was adopted, and I never got the impression they suspected I was a twin. However they might have some knowledge of the adoption agency and why it thought we should be adopted out to different families."

"Look." Simon pointed down the road to a man approaching from the other direction. "That's our church bishop walking toward us. He's heading back from town."

Penelope glanced up and saw a tall, lanky elder with a wispy gray beard striding toward them. As they drew near, she wasn't surprised when the man stared at her. "Sarah? *Was machst du, wenn du so gekleidet bist?*"

Penelope understood the question to say *What are you doing dressed like that?*

Simon interrupted. "*Nein,* this isn't Sarah. She's a guest at the B&B. Penelope Moore, please meet Samuel Beiler, our church leader."

"How do you do?" asked Penelope politely, holding out her hand.

The bishop grasped her hand with an iron grip and peered at her face more closely. "How strange," he murmured.

"*Ja,* it is," Simon replied. "Bishop, the most wondrous thing has happened. Penelope came in as a total stranger to stay at my B&B, and I thought the same thing—how much she looks like Sarah. I arranged for them to meet, and we just returned from visiting. As it turns out, Penelope and Sarah are twin sisters separated at birth."

The older man's jaw dropped. "You're kidding."

"*Nein.* Neither knew the other existed."

"It was quite a surprise," Penelope added with a touch of humor.

"Indeed." The bishop looked, if possible, as dazed as she felt herself. "I've never heard of such a thing."

"We both knew we were adopted," she said, "but apparently our families didn't know about the other sister. If that's the case, the adoption agency is at fault."

"Can you contact the agency?" asked the church leader.

"No, they went out of business years ago. If they split up twins," she added with some sarcasm, "I can understand why."

"*Ja.* Well, Miss Moore, you're more than welcome to our community. I hope you'll stay awhile and have Sarah introduce you around. I'm sure many will be eager to meet you."

"She should come to the church service on Sunday," suggested Simon.

"Of course!" The bishop smiled. "That would be an excellent opportunity to introduce you. Please consider it, Miss Moore."

"Thank you." She smiled with some uncertainty, not quite sure how she felt about the invitation.

The bishop touched the brim of his hat and continued down the road. Penelope and Simon started walking toward the B&B.

"Is that normal?" she inquired. "Asking a perfect stranger to a church service?"

"Well, you're something of an exception," Simon replied. "But he's right in one respect. Once word gets out that you and Sarah are twins, everyone is going to want to meet you. After every church service, we have a potluck meal. It would certainly be the most efficient way to let everyone's curiosity be satisfied."

"Back to feeling like an animal in a zoo, then." But she felt a prickle of curiosity to attend an Amish church service.

"The service will be in German," he warned, "but you said you've studied the language, *ja*?"

"Just as a requirement in high school. We had a choice

of languages and I felt pulled toward German. I got really into it for a while and studied it even after graduating, and even took a trip to visit the country. But it's been so long, I don't know how much I remember."

"You may have the chance to re-learn what you've forgotten, then."

They walked in silence for a few moments.

"I can't wait to call my parents," she remarked at length.

"You said you always had a nagging feeling that something was missing from your life?"

"Yes. Maybe it was an unconscious longing for my sister."

"Perhaps. One thing is certain, it's the hand of *Gott* that made you reserve a stay at my B&B. Of all the places in the country you could have gone to do some painting, why here? *Gott* clearly wanted you to meet Sarah."

Penelope jerked. She was silent a few moments. "I never thought of God one way or the other," she finally admitted. "My parents never discouraged faith by any means, but they never encouraged it, either. I would have called this a coincidence rather than the hand of God, but maybe you're right."

"As a man of faith," Simon replied, "I can see no other explanation. The odds are too astronomical otherwise."

She rubbed her forehead in a gesture of confusion. "You may be right. At any rate, I may have to stay longer here in Montana than originally planned. I... I want to get to know my sister."

"I'll have a room for you as long as you want," he replied.

The moment they returned to the B&B, Penelope

closed herself in her room and pulled out her flip phone. Her hands trembled as she dialed her parents' phone number.

"Hi, Mom," she began when her mother, Angie, answered. "Is Dad there? I have something I need to tell you both."

"Sure," Angie replied, a note of alarm in her voice. "Is everything okay?"

"Yes, I'm fine, but this is important. Please go get Dad."

When her father, Walter, arrived, her mother put Penelope on speaker phone. "What's wrong, honey?"

"Nothing's wrong, just strange." Penelope related how she had arrived and settled into the B&B in Montana. "The owner of the B&B kept telling me how much I looked like his sister-in-law. He went on and on about it, and made arrangements for us to meet, so we did. Mom, Dad, you need to know—she's my identical twin sister."

Her parents gave a collective gasp of shock. "But how…?" her mother began, then trailed off.

"The only thing I can think of is the adoption agency deliberately split us up," said Penelope. "Neither my sister—her name is Sarah—nor I have any idea why, and as far as she knows, her parents also had no idea she was a twin."

Walter gave a low whistle. "When the agency got shut down so many years ago, I heard they were engaged in some unethical practices, but we never imagined it had to do with separating twins. I'm so sorry, honey. If we knew there were two of you, we would not have hesitated to raise you both."

"It's not your fault!" Penelope felt an upwelling of

love for her selfless parents. "You didn't know, and neither did Sarah's parents. In this, we can entirely blame the agency. Another thing you should know—Sarah is Amish. In fact, the B&B where I'm staying is run by an Amish man. I didn't know the church had spread to Montana, but it has."

"Amish." Her mother said the word thoughtfully. "I think I remember hearing that your birth mother was Amish."

"Yes, that's what Sarah understood, too."

"What's she like, your sister?" asked Angie.

"Oh, Mom, she's wonderful!" Penelope gushed. "We look identical. She's married and has two children, and she's just the nicest person. We're looking forward to getting to know each other better."

"What are the odds?" asked Walter rhetorically. "Of all the places you could have randomly gone with this first assignment for your new job, what are the odds you would end up meeting a long-lost twin?"

The hand of God. That's how Simon had phrased it. "The guy who runs the B&B, he said the same thing." She paused. "I might linger a little longer here in Montana than originally planned. I want to get to know Sarah better."

"Of course you should." Angie's voice turned wistful. "I wish we could meet her, too."

"Maybe someday you can." Penelope gave a shaky chuckle. "I almost fainted when I first saw her. It was like looking into a mirror."

She caught her parents up on the rest of her recent developments, and made sure they understood the lack of internet at the B&B. "The phone works, but I can't get email or go online unless I head into town. Dad, do you think you can find anything online about the history of the adoption agency?"

"You bet." Her father's voice was growly, something that happened when he was fighting anger. "It frosts me to think that place deprived you of a lifetime of knowing your twin."

"Well, I've found her now. We can't change the past, but we can do things differently in the future."

She said her goodbyes, then dropped into the rocking chair and stared blindly out at the garden. She could well imagine the intense conversation taking place between her parents now that she was off the line.

She hoped her father would be able to find something about her infancy. In the meantime, she wanted to get to know Sarah better, which meant staying longer at the B&B.

She hesitated. She wasn't in Montana for recreation or even a family reunion. She was here to do business… for a scheme Simon didn't know about. How long could she string out her stay at his B&B without jeopardizing her job?

She supposed she would be finding out soon enough.

Simon sat on a crate before one of the raised garden beds, weeding. He weeded when he was troubled in thought, which was one of the reasons his garden was in such beautiful shape. Since weeds were a constant in any garden, they provided a convenient outlet when he was wrestling with any issues.

Today he dwelled on the reunion between sisters. How could an adoption agency so callously split up twins? Did Penelope and Sarah's birth mother know the fate of her children? What happened to the mysterious Amish girl who had given up her babies and then disappeared from all records? Simon said a silent prayer for the unknown woman.

Meanwhile—and maybe it was the experience of meeting Sarah—it seemed Penelope was as lovely as her sister. Lovelier, in fact, because she seemed more sparkling and vibrant than Sarah.

He heard footsteps crunching on gravel, and glanced over to see Penelope entering the garden.

He rose from the crate. "Did you get hold of your parents?"

"Yes. They were fairly stunned by the news." She ran a hand over her eyes. "They said if they'd had any idea I had a twin, they wouldn't have hesitated to raise us both. My dad is going to do some research to see what he can find out about the adoption agency, but since it shut down so many years ago, I don't know what he'll find."

"Your parents sound like *gut* people."

A smile flitted across her face. "They are. I was very fortunate they adopted me."

"I'm sure Sarah's parents felt the same."

"I wonder if I can meet her parents someday." She looked thoughtful. "It's almost like we're now a more extended family than any of us knew about." She squatted down and started pulling weeds.

"You don't have to do that!" he protested.

"Do what?"

"Weed the garden."

"I don't mind weeding. My mother kept a garden every summer. I'm used to it."

She certainly seemed to know which plants were carrots and which were not. He shrugged. "In that case, let me get you an extra weeder." From the garden shed, he fetched an extra version of the hand tool he preferred to use, as well as another crate to sit on. She sat on the opposite side of the garden bed and extracted weeds with an efficiency he would not have guessed.

She told him about the conversation with her parents. "My father said the same thing as you did," she concluded. "What are the odds of landing here, of all places? The more I think about it, the more I marvel at what a miracle it is."

"And the more I see the hand of *Gott*," he agreed.

"Tell me about the community," she said in a thoughtful voice. "I mean, I grew up in Pennsylvania and saw a lot of Amish people, but I never really knew much about them aside from the basics."

"That's a big question." Simon smiled for a moment. He plucked a weed. "I suppose it's a matter of how much we incorporate our faith into our daily lives. Most people can only see the lack of electricity and then announce they could *never* live that way." His voice took on a wry tone.

"So why *do* you live without electricity?"

He chuckled. "It goes back to 1920, I think, when the church elders made the decision about whether to bring the new technology into our lives. The criterion they use to decide these things is whether it would undermine our community and family structure. Since electricity requires a permanent link to the world, the decision was made not to weaken ties by using electricity. Whenever a new technology appears, a similar decision must be made. Radio, television, the internet…we have to decide how disruptive it would be."

"But you have a website for the business, and a telephone…"

"*Ja*, sure. And I have solar panels, mostly because my guests expect to be able to charge their electronic devices. And many church people have emails, and some other businesses have phones. Sometimes technology is needed to keep our businesses running. It does no good if we can't compete among the *Englisch* and we lose our farms or our livelihood. This is what the church elders must grapple with each time—deciding what technology is allowed that won't harm the cohesion of the community. While we try to live not 'of' the world, we must still live 'in' the world."

"That's why you must go to the library to check your email, right? It's modern technology, but it doesn't impact your daily life."

"Right." He was pleased she understood. "If I carried one of those smart phones in my pocket all the time, it would affect my daily life. If everyone in the community used a smart phone, we would no longer talk to each other or want to work together."

She gave a grim chuckle. "I don't like smart phones. I'm the only one I know who doesn't have one. Too many people get sucked in to them and never lift their heads to see the real world."

"Well, a phone by itself is not bad," he remarked. "Here in Montana, most of us are far separated from family members, and sometimes a phone call is the only way to communicate in case of an emergency. Sarah, for example, could place a phone call to one of the storekeepers in our old hometown, and they would be able to get word to her parents."

"How often do non-Amish people become Amish?"

"Not very often. It's too hard for most people to give up their modern conveniences."

"Yes, I suppose I can see that." She plucked a weed.

"It goes beyond electricity," he added after a moment. "To become Amish means to subsume one's identity to that of the community as an expression of our faith. That's probably the hardest thing of all."

"What do you mean, to subsume one's identity?"

"I mean, we don't identify ourselves as…as…well, by our careers or whatever. Pride of achievement is not an individual thing, it's a community thing. We're all trained from infancy to let our faith show through everything we do. If someone becomes *hochmut*—proud—of something they achieved on their own, it focuses attention on the individual rather than on community accomplishments."

"Yet you started this B&B on your own. You built this beautiful garden on your own. You're not proud of what you've accomplished?"

He winced. He could almost hear his father's criticism, and his own determination to succeed in the face of paternal disapproval. Rather than admit this insecurity, however, he prevaricated. "It's not *hochmut* to work hard and accomplish things. It's not *hochmut* to succeed in a business. It only becomes *hochmut* when that pride of success means we brag, or show off, or disparage others for not achieving similar success, or do anything else that might sow dissent in the community."

She was silent a moment, digging in the dirt. "I can

see how different that is," she admitted after a bit. "The first question most people ask upon meeting someone new is what they do for a living, as if that determines what kind of person they are. But when someone sees an Amish person, the first thing they assume is it doesn't matter what they do for a living, what matters is they're Amish. Am I right?"

"*Ja*, you are!" He was impressed. It was decent insight for an *Englischer*. "Obviously we must all work using the skills and interests *Gott* gives us, but our work doesn't *define* us. Our faith does."

"I wonder…" She poked at the soil. "I wonder how different my life would have been had I been raised Amish with Sarah."

Her voice held a note of poignancy that puzzled him. "It would have been very different," he admitted. "But has it been so bad up until now?"

"No, it hasn't. I think my parents did a good job raising me. But it seems Sarah has something I lack."

"She has faith." To him, that seemed like the most obvious difference.

But the simple sentence seemed to startle her. She stared at him for a moment, then dropped her gaze to the bed of carrots. "I suppose so…"

To Simon, she seemed like a soul in search of a home. "All throughout the Bible," he said quietly, "there are references to seeds. Seeds of faith, seeds as the word of *Gott*, sowing good seed, that kind of thing. But though people can plant and water seeds, only *Gott* can make them grow. Maybe you've just been given a seed."

"And now it's up to God to make it grow?" She gave him a slightly sad smile. "I don't know if it's that easy."

"I never said it was easy. I just said that's how it works."

"So you didn't make this garden grow?" She waved her hand over the entire enclosed area.

"I built the raised beds and filled them with *gut* soil. I fenced it against the deer. I keep the weeds under control. I have a drip irrigation system throughout. But make the seeds grow? *Nein*. I can't do that. No one can."

"On the other hand, the seeds wouldn't have grown if you hadn't done all the prep work."

"*Ja*, true." He grinned. "It's a *gut* partnership between us and *Gott*, *ja*?"

"Yes." She chuckled and rose from the crate. "I'm feeling the urge to get some painting done. God may have given me the talent, but it doesn't do any good until I put brush to canvas."

"Dinner at six," he told her.

"Thank you."

He watched as she threaded her way among the garden beds and slipped through the gate. What an interesting conversation.

He returned to his weeding, but his mind wasn't as troubled. Instead, he felt hopeful. While he couldn't be certain, it seemed he was witnessing the dawning of faith in someone who was lacking it before.

He suspected Sarah might play an influential role in directing Penelope toward *Gott*. It was clear his guest already admired and esteemed her sister. He found himself hoping Sarah could water the seed *Gott* had planted.

And then he wondered why he cared as much as he did.

Chapter Five

❧

Penelope woke up early in the morning with one thought dominating her mind: *I have a sister.* And not just any sister: a twin. After a lifetime of being an only child, it was a thrilling development to know she was not alone. The excitement far overshadowed the gravity of an adoption agency that would split up twins.

"You look happy," Simon observed an hour later, as he served breakfast in the dining room.

"Wouldn't *you* be?" she returned with a smile. "My whole life has altered in the span of a day. I'm still feeling stunned, but in a good way."

Simon chuckled. His eyes crinkled, with laugh lines at the corners highlighted by a shaft of sunlight. She decided he was a handsome man.

"I'm going into town this afternoon to check my email," he said. "I'm also going to take another look at the website my *Englisch* friend designed. I've been thinking it over and you may be right. It could probably be improved."

"I could…" She trailed off. Her first impulse was to offer to help improve the website. She had the skills and experience to beef up his online exposure and his marketing. But that would go counter to what her assignment was from QuirkyB&B. If he improved his website and made some other marketing and advertising changes, he was far less likely to be interested in joining the franchise.

"You could what?" inquired Simon.

"I could get some painting done while you're gone..." she improvised awkwardly.

She broke off at a staccato knock on the front door, followed almost immediately by the door opening. Sarah poked her head inside. *"Guder mariye!"* she called.

"Guder mariye," Penelope and Simon replied together. *"Komm* in," Simon added.

Sarah's dress was dark green with a black apron over the top. Her *kapp* was tidy over her dark hair. She carried a basket over one arm.

"Penelope, I'm going to a quilting party this afternoon," she said as she advanced into the dining room and set her basket on the shelf of the service window. "Would you like to *komm*?"

Penelope felt a moment's uncertainty. "I've never quilted before," she warned. "Will I just be in the way?"

"Nein. There will be many women there and we'll all show you the ropes. I have a feeling," Sarah added, with a sparkle of mischief in her eyes, "you'll be the hit of the party. And if you're interested in getting to know some people in the church community, here's an opportunity."

"Then yes, I'd love to come. Will your children be there, too?"

"Ja, of course. It's an informal quilting bee with mostly younger women, so many will have their children with them. We're going to Eva Hostetler's house."

"How do I get there?"

"If you want to walk over and meet me around one o'clock, we can walk there. I'll pull the children in a wagon." Sarah's gaze shifted to Simon. "I brought you some blueberry jam for your guests. It's last year's jam, but I have to make room in our pantry for this year's crop."

"Danke." Simon reached into the basket and pulled out six pints of jam, then returned the basket to her. "I appreciate it."

"I'll be going, then. Amos is watching the *kinner* at the moment, but he needs to get to work."

Penelope watched as her sister closed the front door behind her. Then she turned to Simon. "I have to resist the feeling of intimidation," she admitted. "She seems so incredibly accomplished. Quilting? Blueberry jam?"

"I assume you have your own accomplishments," he replied, stacking the jars of jam in a cabinet. "Sarah can't paint, for example. But you both seem *gut* at creative things."

"I wonder if I'm *still* going to feel like an animal in a zoo," she mused, finishing the last of the biscuits on her plate. "Everyone staring."

"Ja, probably, at first. It's natural. You'll like this group of women, though. They're all about the same age and with children about the same ages. They meet several times a month and work on quilts either for each other, or as gifts for someone, or sometimes to sell at a store in town. They're nice women, and some of Sarah's closest friends."

Penelope felt a quiver of envy. "I don't have many close friends," she mused, sipping her tea. "I had some while I was growing up, of course, but then I moved to Boston and it was hard to make friends outside of work. And while my coworkers were nice enough, I wasn't close with them." She sighed. "Sarah lives an enviable life."

"Sarah lives the life of an ordinary Amish woman," Simon replied. "That's what I mentioned yesterday about community being the heart of our church. Shared tasks foster friendships. Sarah could make a quilt by herself, but instead she makes a quilt with friends. Meanwhile the children of all the women have a chance to play together, making more friendships."

So that's how it's done. Penelope had to fight off envy at the simple equation. Instead she rose and brought her dishes to the service window. "I'd best get some painting done before going to see her, then. Thank you for breakfast—it was delicious."

She set up her easel in the garden and continued working on the piece she had sketched out the day before, but her mind was buzzing with what Simon related. Meeting Sarah was an amazing thing, but it also diluted her focus and purpose for being here.

"Think of the money," she gritted, and visualized her most recent unpaid credit card bill. She should be concentrating on garnering information on Simon's business, not attending quilting parties.

And yet…she wanted to go. She felt tugged to go. She wanted to get to know Sarah. She wanted to meet other people within the community. Almost—but not quite—she resented this job assignment that interfered with her ability to purely enjoy the opportunities to do so.

But she also promised herself to start working on convincing Simon why franchising his business was a wise thing to do…even though, personally, she thought he didn't need it. From what she had been able to deter-mine so far, his only weakness was on the advertising and marketing side of things, areas where—ironically—she had the most experience.

"Maybe Simon should hire me," she muttered as she packed up her art supplies, returned them to her room and got ready to walk to Sarah's. But she suspected Simon's finances would not permit him to hire a consultant, much less match the generous commission she was promised if her mission here was successful. In other words, fantasy didn't pay the bills.

"Have fun," Simon said and smiled as she bid him goodbye.

She walked the mile to Sarah's house, enjoying the rural scenery and comparing it to the crowded, noisy years of working in Boston. Birdsong instead of traffic horns, solitude instead of crowded sidewalks…she liked it here.

Sarah was outside as Penelope approached the house, holding her daughter and helping her young son into a wagon with high side rails.

"Here, let me hold her," offered Penelope, taking the baby girl from Sarah's arms.

"*Danke.* Here, Paul, climb on in…"

The reaction of both children on seeing someone who resembled their mother was comical, Penelope noted. Little Eleanor stiffened in her arms and prepared to cry, but then she caught her breath and stared at Penelope in confusion. Little Paul climbed into the wagon and appeared not to notice anything amiss until Sarah nestled Eleanor into the wagon with him. Then he saw Penelope's face and drew his eyebrows together. *"Mamm?"* he asked.

"Nein, this is your aunt Penelope," replied Sarah. "Isn't it fun? She looks like me, *ja*?"

"Ja," the boy replied, staring. He glanced between his mother and Penelope, then smiled.

She grinned back at the child. "Hello, Paul." Instinct told her not to push further until the boy felt more comfortable with her.

Sarah tucked a diaper bag into the wagon with the children, then seized the handle. "Ready?"

"Yes." Penelope fell into step beside her sister. "Tell me about Amos. How long have you been married?"

"It will be six years next month. Ach, he's a *gut* man." Sarah's eyes softened. *"Gott* has blessed me with a wonderful helpmeet. I… I… Well, I'm expecting again. Soon the *kinner* will have another sibling."

"Oh, Sarah, that's wonderful!" Penelope threw an arm around Sarah's shoulders and gave her a quick hug.

"No one else knows except Amos, so please don't mention it yet. But I'm happy."

"You *seem* happy."

Sarah gave her a sharp glance. "And you're not?"

"It's not that. It's just…well, I confess I envy you a bit." In fact, Penelope found herself envying her newfound sister *a lot.* She was surprised by the sharp longing for the domestic felicity Sarah seemed to enjoy so effortlessly.

"'For where envying and strife is, there is confusion and every evil work,'" murmured Sarah.

"What's that?"

"Oh, just one of my favorite Bible verses. It talks about the pitfalls of envy."

"Hmm." Penelope was silent a moment. "Yet it seems envy fuels so much in modern society, doesn't it?"

"I suppose so. It's one of the reasons I don't live among

the *Englisch*. I don't envy envy," Sarah concluded with a chuckle.

"Sarah…" Penelope hesitated. "Have you ever felt a dull, nagging sense of loss or something missing?"

Sarah looked startled. "*Nein*. Why?"

"Because it's something I've felt for as long as I could remember. When I met you yesterday I wondered if it stemmed from an unconscious longing for a sister I never knew I had, but here you are and I still feel it. Just wondering what's wrong with me, I guess."

"Have you tried praying about it?"

"Praying?" Penelope repeated the word as if she'd never heard it before. "No."

"You might try it. It works whenever I'm troubled over something."

The utter simplicity of the suggestion baffled Penelope. Did prayer actually work? She had her doubts.

But any thoughts of prayer fled as they approached a pretty two-story house with a fenced yard. Several children played in the yard—the girls in pastel dresses with miniature *kapps* and aprons, the boys in dark trousers, suspenders and bright-colored shirts. The children ran and shrieked, creating a happy jumble of movement.

"*Komm* and meet Eva and my other friends," invited Sarah, reaching in to unlatch the yard gate and pulling the wagon through. Little Paul immediately climbed out and ran to join the other boys. "I know you're going to cause a stir."

Penelope suspected that was an understatement.

Sarah lifted her daughter from the wagon and settled the toddler on her hip. Penelope carried the diaper bag and followed her sister toward the house. The front door was open, but Sarah led the way behind the house to where a quilting frame was set up under the shade of a generous fir tree. Penelope heard a subdued hum of women's voices chatting quietly in German.

One woman looked up. *"Guten tag,* Sarah. *Wie ghets..."* Her voice trailed off. Gradually all the voices ceased as eight women all looked up and stared at Penelope. She smiled, trying not to act intimidated at the sudden quiet.

Sarah spoke into the stunned silence. "I'd like you all to meet Penelope Moore," she said in English. "She's a guest at Simon's B&B. We only met each other yesterday and found we are twin sisters separated at birth."

The brief explanation set off a huge reaction from the other women. They jerked out of their seats, leaving needles dangling from the quilt by the threads, and crowded around Penelope and Sarah. *"Das ist erstaunlich!" "Unglaublich! Ein wunder!"*

Penelope remembered enough German to understand their exclamations, and she laughed at the outpouring of welcome. *"Danke!"* she said over and over.

One woman detached herself. She had warm blue eyes. "I'm Eva Hostetler," she said. "This is our home. You're most *welkom*, Penelope."

"Thank you. It was quite a shock to learn Sarah and I are sisters, I can assure you."

"Are you joining us in quilting?"

"Yes, if you don't mind a novice who has never quilted before. You'll have to tell me what I'm doing."

"Of course. Here, sit by me. Gracious, you two look so identical, I can't get over it."

Sarah seated herself and threaded a needle, which she handed over the quilt top to Penelope. "This part of quilting is easy," she said. "But it's kind of boring, which is why quilting parties are the best way to get it done. See how we're stitching the quilt top to the back? All you have to do is follow these lines…"

Penelope listened carefully as her sister explained how to guide the needle through the top of the fabric with her dominant hand and redirect it from below with her nondominant hand. After a few practice stitches, during which Eva offered a pointer or two, she was soon sewing companionably with the rest.

It was a revelation to be with a group of women focusing on a single goal, casually gossiping about daily lives without an ounce of cattiness, with children wandering in and out of the vicinity. Even Sarah's tiny daughter toddled on the grass and played with some of the toys Eva had brought out. Once in a while a woman would be pulled away to attend to a scraped knee or a request for snacks, but otherwise the swarm of children largely policed themselves.

"So you had no idea you were a twin?" asked Eva, and the other women paused in their conversation to listen to Penelope's answer.

"No," she replied. "I couldn't understand why Simon kept insisting I meet Sarah. When I did, well…"

"I nearly fainted," confirmed Sarah with a smile. "Imagine looking into a mirror that wasn't a mirror."

Penelope gave a brief explanation of her history, and said her parents were looking into the now-defunct adoption agency to see what they could learn. "But in the end, I doubt anyone will ever know why they decided to split us up," she concluded.

"I hope you can stay a long time and get to know everyone," Eva said.

Penelope hesitated. "I'm technically here for work," she confessed. "I… I'm an artist and often travel to different places to paint. It was sheer chance that I ended up here."

"Sounds like *Gott* had something to do with it," Eva chuckled.

"That's how Simon put it. And Sarah, too." Penelope knew better than to mention her own lack of faith to the women. "Your bishop invited me to church tomorrow. He said everyone will want to meet me. I just wasn't sure how welcome an outsider would be to a service."

"Oh, you'd be very *welkom*!" exclaimed Eva, and a chorus of feminine voices agreed with her.

"I'll feel kind of funny in regular clothes, though." Penelope plucked at her blouse.

"Unless…" Eva's eyes twinkled. "Unless we dress you in Amish clothing."

As the implications dawned on the rest of the group, a ripple of laughter spread among them.

"Ja!" exclaimed Sarah. "I have a dress and apron and *kapp* you can use. I mean, what's the fun of having a twin if you can't play around a bit?"

Penelope got into the spirit of things. "I won't get in trouble for, I don't know, impersonating an Amish woman or something?"

"Certainly not," retorted Sarah with a grin. "Besides, by this time tomorrow a lot of church members will know I have a twin. But what if they can't tell us apart?"

"Except for the language barrier," replied Penelope. *"Ich spreche etwas Deutsch*—I speak some German— but it's been years and I don't remember much."

"That's okay. *Bitte*, Penelope? It would be such fun."

"Okay," she replied. "I'm game if you are."

Two hours later, Penelope found herself back at Sarah's. The tired children went down for naps, after which Sarah practically dragged Penelope upstairs to her bedroom.

"What color do you prefer?" she asked. She pulled several garments off hooks. "Green? Burgundy? Blue?"

"The burgundy is lovely." Penelope touched one of the dresses.

"Try it on," Sarah urged.

Within minutes, Penelope found herself attired in the dress and apron. "Next, shoes and stockings," said Sarah. "I don't normally wear these except to church, since I prefer sandals during the summer. But you can wear them home." Her eyes crinkled with mischief. "Simon will definitely think you're me when you show up dressed like this."

"What about the headpiece?" Penelope eyed Sarah's hair covering.

"The *kapp*." Sarah reached into a drawer and pulled out a spare.

"Why do you wear these, anyway?" Penelope took the starched head covering and examined it. "I mean, it's pretty, but…"

"We don't wear it because it's pretty." Sarah smiled. "We're instructed in the Bible to keep our heads covered and sacred to *Gott*. It's also an act of modesty to hide our hair. I'm glad yours is long—that will make it easy. Here's how you'll want to pin it up…"

Under her sister's guidance, Penelope pinned her hair into a bun and slipped the *kapp* over her head. She gave a nervous chuckle. "It almost makes me feel, I don't know…holy?"

"*Ja*, it's supposed to." Sarah grinned. "I know I feel unclothed if I'm not wearing one."

Finally Penelope stood back. "How do I look?"

"Like my twin sister." Sarah hugged her, then drew back, wiping a bit of moisture from her eyes. "I wish you were Amish, Penelope. Then you could stay here."

"I want to stay longer than I planned." Penelope bit her lip, thinking about what excuse she could give QuirkyB&B about why she needed to linger in this remote Montana location. Since it was her first assignment, she suspected such a request would be frowned upon. "Maybe I could sell a bunch of my paintings," she joked weakly.

"I just hate the thought of losing you so soon after finding you."

"I asked Simon how many people convert to Amish," remarked Penelope. "He said not many do, and those that try often don't stick it out."

"*Ja*, I suppose that's true." Sarah bit her lip. "Though personally I can't imagine being anything else."

Just then Penelope heard the sound of a baby crying. "Huh, she didn't nap for very long," remarked Sarah. "Sometimes that happens when she's overtired. I need to get dinner started anyway. Go on, go back to the B&B and I'll see you at church tomorrow."

"Let's see if Simon mistakes me for you, now that I'm dressed this way." Penelope chuckled.

"Grab your *Englisch* clothes," instructed Sarah, heading for the bedroom door. "I have a bag downstairs you can use to carry them back."

Penelope followed her sister downstairs, stuffed her street clothes into the bag, kissed Sarah goodbye and started down the road to the B&B.

It felt exotic being dressed in Amish clothing. Penelope felt as if she was playacting. A part of her was nervous at the thought of meeting someone coming back from town without Sarah or Simon at her side to explain, but this close to dinner the road was deserted and she saw no one.

She walked up the porch steps to the B&B and quietly entered the building. Hearing noises come from the kitchen, she went through the lobby and into the dining room. Sure enough, Simon was cooking. She could see him concentrating on his task through the service window.

"I'm back," she announced, then waited for his reaction.

He looked up. "*Gut*, because I'm making…" His voice trailed off and he stared at her.

Penelope chuckled at his expression. "Sarah loaned me some clothing," she explained. "She and the other women at the quilting session thought it would be fun for me to dress the part when I go to church tomorrow."

He gave a low whistle. "It will be the talk of the community." His eyes twinkled. "You realize it's not the Amish way to draw attention to yourself? I'm surprised Sarah dressed you up."

"It wasn't just her," Penelope said hastily. "All the other women thought so, too."

"Well, if all the other women were in on it, it probably won't be a surprise to many at church. I'm sure the gossip is spreading like wildfire even as we speak. How did you enjoy the quilting, by the way?"

How could she answer that question? It was a revelation to her. Not just the sewing, but the camaraderie, the friendliness, the teasing and the gentle gossip, the children playing… In her mind's eye, she wanted to recreate the scene on canvas.

"It was fun," she summarized. "A lot of fun. I hope I can do something like that again while I'm here."

"I'm sure you can." Simon nodded toward the table where she usually sat. "I've got dinner ready if you're hungry. I'm also baking cookies, both for tomorrow's after-church potluck and for dessert tonight. And, if you don't mind some company, I have something I wanted to talk over with you."

"Of course." She was surprised. "Let me go drop my regular clothes upstairs and I'll be right down."

"You're not going to change?"

She caught a look on his face, one of burgeoning interest, and it made her intrigued. Would dressing Amish change how he interacted with her?

"No," she said with an impish grin. "It's kind of fun to dress differently. You don't mind, do you?"

"*Nein.* I don't mind."

Yes, he was decidedly treating her differently. A barrier had dropped—and she liked it.

She walked up to her room, dropped her regular clothes on the bed and used the bathroom to wash up a bit before dinner. In the mirror, she saw another woman. She saw Sarah, demurely attired with the modesty *kapp* and Plain dress and apron. She touched the *kapp*. Quite honestly, she enjoyed the change.

Chapter Six

Simon didn't want to admit how much it shook him to see Penelope dressed in Amish clothing. It threatened to tear down a barrier that he knew good and well still existed.

He supposed he couldn't blame Sarah for suggesting the swap. What twin could resist the urge to play games with their appearances, especially twins who only just discovered each other? No, it was just an issue of clamping down on his own reaction. Dressed correctly, it was too easy to imagine Penelope was a member of the church. From there it was too easy to engage in a long-term train of thought that couldn't happen.

He firmed his lips and went about setting the table for two. By the time Penelope came back downstairs, he had composed himself. He slipped some cookies into the oven to bake for tomorrow's after-church potluck and set a timer.

"What did you make for dinner?" she inquired as she seated herself.

"Baked chicken and a broccoli casserole." He placed some dishes on hot pads on the table, poured the iced tea he knew she preferred with her meals and sat down opposite. He bowed his head for a silent blessing.

After a few moments, he raised his head and found Penelope staring at him.

"Were you…praying?" she inquired timidly.

"*Ja* sure, of course," he replied. "Before every meal we thank *Gott* for the food."

"I suppose I should start doing that," she mused. "Just another thing I never really learned growing up."

"You'll see everyone doing it at tomorrow's potluck after church. Here, please help yourself." He offered her tongs to serve herself some chicken. "So I wanted to ask you about my business website," he began.

"Of course." She finished filling her plate.

"I went into town this afternoon to check my email," he said. "I have two guest reservations, which was nice to see. One is an overnight stay. The other is a week-long stay. Then I did something I hadn't done in a while. I got onto the website my *Englisch* friend had made, and I looked it over carefully. Even with my limited experience with such things, it struck me as…well, uninteresting. I thought I'd ask if you had any ideas for improving it." He took a bite of chicken.

She hesitated, then nodded. "I'm not an expert in building websites," she said, "though I've done it using free website builders. But it strikes me your issue goes beyond just a website and into the whole marketing and advertising side of things. Where do you advertise?"

"Well, the local Chamber of Commerce has me listed…"

She waited, but he had nothing else to add. "That's all?" she asked.

"At the moment, *ja*." He tried not to feel defensive. "Up to this point, the vast majority of my efforts went into fixing up the house and grounds. I haven't put much into the marketing and advertising. I... I don't know how."

"But I do." She chewed a bite of food. "That's what I did before I got laid off from my job and decided to become a full-time artist. Your place is certainly off the beaten track, so you'd need to capitalize on that and turn it to your advantage. Being off-grid is a novelty for those who might be jaded with the technology of city life. And the fact that you serve meals made of things you grow yourself or obtain from other church members is a huge selling point." She hefted her fork. "This is delicious."

"Danke." He felt some frustration welling inside him. "But how do I advertise all those things? How can I get the word out about the unique aspects of my business? I realize I should have thought of all this sooner, but I was just so tied up in the construction aspect that it got pushed aside."

"Obviously both sides of starting a business are important. You can't have one without the other. Fortunately you already have the hard part done, which is the construction of the house and garden. The marketing side is easily remedied."

He had to resist the urge to beg for her help. After all, the very last thing he wanted to do was admit to his *daed* that he had failed.

Into the momentary silence, she asked, "How have your customers found you up to this point? I was looking for a rural location for my art, but what about your other customers? How did you connect with them?"

"Mostly the people who have stayed here had friends or family in the area," he said. "The local *Englisch* high school had its graduation a couple months ago, and several people came to town to attend that. I've had people stay who were here to witness a wedding. Once or twice I had someone here on business."

"But how did they hear of you?"

"Mostly through the Chamber of Commerce, but also through word of mouth. There's another Amish-run business in town, a boardinghouse that often gets full during community events. He sends any overflow guests my way. That's what I mean by word of mouth."

She grimaced. "That's not a very aggressive strategy."

"I know that." He wasn't sure whether to feel annoyed or defensive. "Now that I'm fully open for business and have the garden up and running, I'm in a position to increase the number of bookings."

"Except for the construction in your personal quarters." A glint of mischief shone in her eyes as she gestured toward the back of the house.

The tension eased and he chuckled. "*Ja* sure, but I can work on that in my free time. It's low on my priority list." He sobered. "But now that full summer is here, I need to take advantage of any tourism in the area or visitors passing through. Not to mention attracting a demographic which, as you suggest, might want an off-grid experience to balance their high-tech lifestyle."

"One of the first things you'll need to do is optimize your SEO, your search engine optimization," she said.

"What's that?" he asked, bewildered.

"It's a means of allowing anyone doing an online search to find you. The idea is to use location-based keywords and keyword phrases to capture traffic from those looking for a stay near you. Your business website would be the first to come up."

She might as well have been speaking a foreign language. He couldn't understand a word she was saying. For a moment, despair clutched at him. It seemed too overwhelming to learn.

But an idea struck him. "If you would be interested in helping with the marketing side of things," he said slowly, "I could discount your stay here. It would also give you a chance to stay longer and get to know Sarah better."

He thought it was a reasonable offer. What he didn't expect was panic to drench her face. "I c-can't," she stuttered.

"Can't what?" he asked. "Stay longer?"

"Partly, yes. But I can't help you with the marketing. It's, um, not my strong point."

"But you just said that's what you did in your last job before you got laid off." He was genuinely confused.

But his confusion was nothing in the face of her outright alarm. She suddenly had the look of a trapped animal, and he couldn't figure out why. Was his offer so unorthodox?

"I j-just can't," she stuttered.

So he did the only thing he could do. He backed off. The last thing he wanted to do was chase her away. "Not a problem," he said. "I can talk to some people in town and get ideas. I'm sorry, Penelope, I didn't mean to put you on the spot."

She nodded and took a sip of tea, still looking wary.

After a few moments of silence, she said unexpectedly, "I'm grateful to you, Simon. If it wasn't for you, I would never have known I had a twin, much less ever had a chance to meet her."

"Then perhaps…" He paused and decided to voice something that had been more and more on his mind. "Perhaps you should work to overcome whatever obstacles are preventing you from staying longer and getting to know Sarah better." *And me*, he thought.

"I wonder if I could." She spoke thoughtfully. "Meeting Sarah was a game changer."

"What about…" He stopped suddenly and resisted the urge to clap a hand over his mouth.

She looked at him. "What about what?"

"Nothing." Not for anything would he admit he was about to say, *What about me?* It was easier to admit he was interested in having her stay longer as more than simply a chance to get to know her twin. He wanted her to stay longer to get to know *him*.

Feeling awkward, Simon changed the subject. "So I have these new guests arriving early next week," he remarked. "You'll have more company in the dining room now than just myself."

His weak attempt at a joke fell flat as she hardly acknowledged his quip. "That will be nice," she mumbled, looking at her plate.

What had he said to change her mood? Was it his offer to discount her stay in exchange for marketing help?

It was with enormous relief that he heard the timer in the kitchen go off. "Excuse me, I've got cookies in the oven." He rose from the table and busied himself removing cookies from the oven and sliding them onto cooling racks. Meanwhile he kept a discreet eye on Penelope.

She finished her dinner and brought the dishes to

the service window. "Thank you, that was delicious," she said. "What time do I need to be ready for church tomorrow?"

"About nine thirty. I'll have breakfast ready at eight."

He watched as she nodded and left the dining room. In fact, *fled* might be a better word. He was still puzzled at her sudden withdrawal.

Then he chided himself. His interest in her—especially dressed as she was—was exceeding his duties as a host. Her moods were none of his business, nor should he have requested professional assistance from her. He had certainly never treated any of his other guests inappropriately. Why was Penelope different?

Or *was* he treating her inappropriately? He knew he wasn't. What he was doing was treating her like a beautiful woman he wanted to know better. And that, he knew, was a problem.

Well, one thing was certain. Going forward, he would treat her with the same degree of professional hospitality he had always extended to his other guests. He would not seek her out for intimate conversations over meals... even though he enjoyed them immensely.

He had no option. Despite her playing dress-up, she wasn't Amish. He *had* to remember that.

Penelope escaped upstairs to her room, furious with herself. How could she have admitted to her background in marketing? How had she let herself be drawn into a conversation about improving Simon's online presence? How could she have suggested improvements to the B&B in the very area where his business was weak?

His lack of online presence and poor marketing was

what brought him to the attention of QuirkyB&B in the first place. She was here to convince Simon to come under their umbrella, not help him succeed on his own.

He was turning into a friend rather than a professional subject to be investigated, and that wasn't what she was here to do.

She picked up her latest credit card bill and glared at it. This piece of paper represented her motivation for being here.

When she was laid off at her marketing position three months ago, the financial blow was doubled when her apartment rent skyrocketed. It left her financially reeling. She'd been forced to put not one, but two months' worth of rent on her credit card—with no means in sight of paying it off.

QuirkyB&B and its promise of a hefty commission for bringing in new clients was her salvation for paying off the bill. She couldn't—wouldn't—do anything that would compromise that hope.

Penelope hated debt. Her parents had struggled financially during her teenage years, and didn't have the financial means to send her to college. They also urged her to pursue a career without burdening herself with student loans from a college degree, and she had managed to secure an internship at the marketing company in Boston and learn the trade. But the lack of a professional degree also made her one of the first to be laid off when business contracted.

All those years of being diligent about her finances came crashing down when she couldn't find another job in Boston that paid well enough—until she connected with QuirkyB&B.

The QuirkyB&B job was the perfect match for her skills, and an ideal solution to her housing situation. Not only would she be mobile and not have to pay rent, but her commissions would earn her enough to pay off the thousands of dollars she owed on her credit card.

She slammed the offensive bill onto the nightstand and dropped into the rocking chair, staring out at the garden. It was the "golden hour," when the lowering sun cast the most beautiful shadows among the vegetables. Gradually her emotions, tied in knots of frustration, loosened and relaxed.

She thought about the quilting party she had attended. Maybe it was just her physical resemblance to Sarah, but she had felt very much at home and welcomed by the other women. It was an extraordinary feeling. Penelope couldn't ever remember feeling that kind of simple acceptance. She wondered if Sarah realized how unusual that was.

Or maybe it wasn't that unusual for Sarah. Maybe that's just the way it was for her every day.

A vision formed in Penelope's mind: a painting of a quilting party. Women, their heads covered in white *kapps*, bent over their work. A colorful quilt held flat on a quilting frame. Grass beneath, the shade from a tree above, children playing, a house in the background…

Yes, she could visualize the painting in its final form. It was up to her to put it on canvas.

She rose from the rocking chair and reached for her sketchbook and pencil. She outlined the scene on paper, being sure to incorporate the golden ratio and rule of thirds for artistic composition in the position of the tree over the quilting frame.

Oh, this would make a lovely painting. She itched to get started on it.

She stood up and sorted through her canvases. Finally she took the largest—two by three feet—and set it upon the easel in the corner. The light was still bright enough to lightly sketch with the pencil on canvas the outline of what she wanted to paint.

As she added details, she thought about the intense experiences of the last few days. She had expected her first assignment from QuirkyB&B to be straightforward. Instead she got distractions she never expected. A new sister, a new family, a new community that welcomed her. If she was truthful, she wished she could stop living a lie. She wished she *was* here just for her art. Life would be so much simpler.

The grip on her pencil tightened. Debt had a habit of enslaving. That's what her parents had taught her, and it was true. While she felt grateful to QuirkyB&B for hiring her when they did, her only reason to work for them was to pay off that shackling financial obligation.

The sun slipped beneath mountains to the west and her room became shadowed. Penelope put her pencil down and examined the sketch on canvas. She smiled. Tomorrow she would get started applying color and making the painting come to life.

No, tomorrow she would be attending church with her newfound family and meeting the community members who were so important to her sister. The painting would have to wait, at least until later in the afternoon.

Church. Penelope returned to the rocking chair and watched the shadows creep over the garden. It would be a strange experience, attending church with a group as devout as the Amish. Would she learn anything?

Resting on the bedside table was a Bible. Penelope was familiar with the most common stories of the world's most famous book, but had never really read anything more than bits and pieces. Idly she leafed through the tissue-thin pages, stopping here and there to read. Impulsively she closed her eyes, opened the book to a random page and plopped her finger down. Then she opened her eyes and peered at the verse she had tagged. "The rich ruleth over the poor, and the borrower is servant to the lender."

Her stared at the verse and felt a chill run down her spine. *The borrower is servant to the lender...*

Isn't that what she was experiencing? She had borrowed on her credit card to pay her rent, and now she was bound with a legal obligation to the lender to pay it back, even to the point of deceiving a good man like Simon about her reason for being here.

She leaned back in the rocking chair, the open Bible in her lap, and stared blindly at the shadowed garden. She was here to pay off her debt. Convincing Simon to come under the QuirkyB&B label was just the means to the end.

It seemed like a simple and straightforward arrangement, but literally the moment she showed up—when Simon mistook her for Sarah—things had become a lot more complicated. Her interest in investigating Simon's business was decreasing as her connections to the community increased.

If she were honest with herself, it wasn't just Sarah. It was Simon. He intrigued her as no man ever had before.

There was something about him—a goodness that was different from any other man she had met before. The subtle change in attitude toward her while dressed in Amish garb hinted at the potential for something much deeper…except she didn't dare encourage him.

But sitting here in Amish garb felt remarkably good. She touched the *kapp* on her head and thought about what Sarah had said of its purpose. It was true she felt just a bit purer wearing it, or perhaps it was just her imagination.

But playacting didn't pay the bills. Deceiving Simon would. And that, she realized, didn't sit well on her conscience. He was too fine a man to mislead.

That in itself didn't bode well for the success of her mission. How could she sway such a good man to do something he clearly didn't want to do, solely for her personal benefit? It was an ugly question, and one she had avoided asking until now.

The reason, she realized, is because Simon was rapidly becoming more than just a means to an end. He was becoming more than just a friend.

A movement caught her eye. Below her window, she saw Simon walking in the garden. It was too dark for him to be weeding, and he wasn't watering anything. Instead, he wandered slowly among the beds, his hands clasped behind his back, examining the plants. Sometimes he raised his head to the sky, scanning the dark trees around the property and the silhouette of the distant mountains to the west.

For some reason her throat closed up. She was clearly spying on him during a private moment of reflection, but it seemed he was communing with the garden in a way she didn't understand.

He's praying. The words entered her mind like a voice speaking in her ear.

Was that what he was doing?

What did someone like Simon pray about?

A possible answer rose smooth and unprompted to her mind. Could he be praying for clarity about…her?

For the first time she thought about the implication of the growing attraction between her and Simon. In her world, two people who had an interest in each other could date. It was as simple as that.

But for a devout Amish man, it was not as easy—not when she didn't share his faith.

And faith wasn't something she could just switch on. Or could she?

It seemed prayer came easily to the people around here. She supposed that made sense; the Amish were known for their genuine piety. It just felt…foreign to her.

And yet, there's no question that Bible verse had spoken to her in a way that was entirely unexpected and perhaps just a tiny bit frightening. Of the tens of thousands of verses in the Bible, how was it she put her finger on the exact one that spoke to her situation?

And what other wisdom was contained in the tiny print of that dense tome?

Simon continued to stroll around the garden beds. She knew he couldn't see her in the darkened room, and she took the opportunity to watch him. He wore no hat, though he usually did when he was outdoors. His curly hair looked almost black in the twilight. His features, though shadowed, seemed peaceful.

That sense of peace tugged at her. It was something that had been conspicuously lacking during much of her adult professional life, yet Simon had cultivated that very thing here in his modest B&B. No wonder the kind of financial success that most people craved held little appeal to Simon.

It was clear he wanted his business to succeed, but it was also clear he was determined to do so on his own terms. Somehow she knew her purpose here was doomed to failure. Unless Simon's business was in imminent danger of failing—and it wasn't—she couldn't see convincing him a franchise would be an improvement.

But she had to try. That credit card bill lying on the bedside table seemed to accuse her somehow. *The borrower is servant to the lender...*

She signed and turned away from the window. Her thoughts were unanchored and chaotic, and she wondered what it would take to cultivate the same peaceful mien as Simon had. Or her sister. Or her sister's husband. Or the women she met today at the quilting bee.

What was their secret? She suspected avoiding debt was part of it. But was there more? Was it their church services? Their friendships? Their families?

She didn't know. But she wanted to find out. And maybe, just maybe, Simon was the one who could show her the way.

Chapter Seven

"Do I look okay?" Penelope smoothed down her apron.

"You look fine," Simon said in a calm voice.

"I feel like a fraud, dressed this way." She touched her *kapp*. "Maybe I shouldn't be wearing Sarah's clothes."

"Everyone knows you're *Englisch*." Simon tucked another insulated food carrier into the basket he was packing for the after-church potluck. "While they might be surprised to see you dressed in Amish clothes, I'm sure they'll just be interested in meeting you."

"Do I understand that men and women sit on opposite sides of the room during the service?"

"*Ja*. I imagine Sarah will have you sit with her." He lifted an eyebrow. "Why are you so nervous?"

"I don't know." She pressed a hand to her midsection. "I suppose I don't want to bring shame to Sarah among her people."

"You won't. Relax." He grinned. "That said, be prepared for a whole lot of covert looks during the service. It's not often we get identical twins out here. There are none in this new church community, though we had a couple pairs in our old church."

"Back to being in a fishbowl," she remarked, though

she couldn't help but be pleased this time. She was still adjusting to the idea of having a duplicate of herself walking around.

Simon hefted the basket off the kitchen counter. "I'm ready to go. Are you?"

"Yes."

"I've got the buggy hitched up."

"Buggy!" Her eyebrows shot up. "We're traveling by buggy?"

"*Ja*, sure. The service is being held at the Stoltzfus farm, and it's a bit far to walk."

"Let's go! I've never traveled by buggy." Suddenly the day seemed almost glamorous, if such a description could apply to a Plain conveyance.

Simon chuckled and led the way outside. Sure enough, a horse with a shining brown coat stood patiently hitched to an open-topped buggy.

Simon hefted the basket of food in the back. "Do you need help getting in?"

"I'll let you know." Penelope examined the vehicle. A small drop-step was folded down on the side. She hitched up the unfamiliar skirt and managed to climb in without embarrassing herself too much. She turned and seated herself. "Ta-da!"

He laughed outright. "Not bad for an *Englischer*." He went behind the buggy and climbed in the other side. Taking the reins and clucking to the horse, he started down the road.

Penelope stayed silent, watching his confident hands handling the reins. The novelty of traveling at a sedate trot behind a horse through beautiful rural farmland was a treat by itself.

It was also a novelty to travel with Simon. It made her feel very connected to him, almost as if…well, as if they were a married couple. It was an interesting thought.

"You shouldn't be surprised by the lack of chatter or visiting before the service," he said at length. "It's a bit more of a solemn time, coming together for worship. Socializing happens afterward."

"I see." Penelope was jolted out of her reverie by the realization that this wasn't a social call. It was a church service. These people took worship very seriously, and it behooved her to approach the day with decorum. "Are we allowed to talk, or is everything silent?"

"Of course we talk!" Simon shot her a surprised glance. "We're just not *noisy*, at least before church. Children are taught to behave themselves, which can be a little hard on the littlest ones who want to wiggle. But afterward, the *kinner* run off and play together, the adults all visit, we have a *gut* meal and thank *Gott* for the pleasure of living in a community where we can come together to worship."

"It sounds lovely." And it did. Penelope had never attended church with enough frequency to get to know anyone. She wondered if the lure of shared worship was a strong enough glue to hold a community together.

"Look, there's the Yoder family." Simon pointed discreetly at a buggy pulling into the road ahead of them. "And I see the Kings as well. That's the Hostetlers over there."

As he indicated, the gravel road saw an uptick in traffic as buggies made their way in the same direction. Gradually she saw people walking, too, which meant the destination was closer.

"The Stoltzfus farm is just ahead." Simon gestured toward where a large house and barn could be glimpsed through the pine trees. "They were the first to have a house and barn big enough to host a church service, so for the longest time we met only there. Now we have two other families on the rotation, so the Stoltzfuses no longer have the solo burden. During the warmer months we meet for worship in the barn."

"I remember reading that you don't have church buildings, right?"

"*Ja.* When our church first formed back in the 1600s, we were persecuted and forced to meet in secret. Services were held in homes, the forest, even in caves. This was a time when churches in Europe were huge and ornate, and seldom used except once a week. After the persecution ended and our ancestors could meet without fear, we just continued to use people's homes for services. That's why so many Amish homes are very large."

"And all this time I thought it was because they had so many children." Penelope grinned.

He smiled back, a touch of mischief on his face. "That, too." He looked very handsome with the glint of humor in his eyes.

He pulled the horse into a driveway. The tunnel of trees cleared and Penelope found herself among the largest group of Amish people she had ever seen. Men unhitched horses, women gathered picnic baskets and babies, children darted among their elders. As Simon had indicated, talk was subdued and an air of solemnity was present.

She received some startled looks. "I have a feeling

some people are wondering why you're arriving with Sarah," she ventured.

"*Ja*, no doubt you're right." He pointed. "And there's Sarah and Amos, just arriving. Now the fun begins!" He grinned.

With a complete lack of grace, Penelope climbed down from the wagon and went to join Sarah. Her sister was dressed in a dark blue dress, in contrast to the wine-colored dress she had loaned Penelope. Sarah gave her a hug. "You look like a proper Amish woman."

"I told Simon I feel like a fraud." She smiled as Amos came up. "Good morning, Amos."

Her brother-in-law smiled. "*Guder mariye.* Wow, you look remarkably alike." He handed her a large hamper. "Would you mind carrying this since Sarah has the baby? I'll go park the buggy."

"Of course." She took the basket and looked at her sister.

"Follow me," invited Sarah. She hoisted the baby on her hip and took Paul's hand.

Walking through the growing clusters of people was like walking through a movie set, where conversation died and crowds parted. People simply stared—not with hostility, but simple amazement. Penelope smiled nervously.

Ahead was a line of picnic tables upon which many baskets and hampers were placed. "We'll unpack these after church," said Sarah.

Penelope hefted the hamper onto one of the tables, then trailed Sarah toward the barn. Inside the spacious building, benches had been set up at angles with an aisle down the middle. Women congregated on one side, men on the other. Some books were scattered on the benches.

"Stay with me until *Daed* arrives," Sarah told her young son in German. "Then you can sit with him. You're to stay quiet, young man, do you understand?"

"Ja, Mamm," the boy replied.

"I actually understood that," remarked Penelope. "I took German in school, but haven't spoken it in years. I think I'm going to have to brush up on it again."

Sarah made her way in among the women, picked up one of the books and sat down, patting the bench next to her to invite Penelope to follow. "It would be helpful, *ja*, if you're going to spend any time with us. I hope the service isn't too boring for you, since it will be in German. Paul, there's your *daed*, you may go to him now," she added to her son.

Penelope glanced over and saw Amos and Simon, who seated themselves opposite. Amos took Paul on his knee.

She glanced at the book Sarah held. "Is that a Bible?"

"Nein, it's an *Ausbund*. An Amish hymnal. It has no musical notes, just the words to various hymns."

More people came crowding in. The air was filled with subdued chatter as people got settled. Penelope sat quietly and observed.

But then everyone started to sing hymns, and Penelope's whole world shifted. Chills went down her spine.

It wasn't that the music was overly professional. It was sung without musical instruments, and often the men sang harmony while the women sang melody, creating absolute beauty within the humble confines of the barn. The songs were slow and incredibly moving.

Beside her, Sarah sang with gusto, holding the *Ausbund* open in her lap. Penelope could see the words were in German, and since she was unfamiliar with the tunes, she made no effort to join in. Instead, she just let the haunting beauty wash over her.

After a time, the bishop stood up and the singing stopped. He began some prayers in German, read some passages in scripture, then launched into a sermon.

For the life of her, she couldn't understand what the church leader was saying. For one thing, the Pennsylvania Dutch dialect was different than the German she had learned in school. For another, he spoke rapidly, his voice soft but full of power. Penelope gave up trying to frantically interpret in her mind, and just let the language wash over her, much as she did the music.

And it almost worked. She caught passages here and there, enough to give her food for thought during the service. She caught the word *schulden*—debt. She wished she could understand more. Beside her, Sarah sat in rapt attention, her daughter asleep on her shoulder, her eyes on the bishop. Penelope envied her sister the pure understanding and familiarity with what was being said.

After the sermon, several other older men stood to speak, though she didn't understand what they were saying. Then every head bowed for a final prayer.

It was during this prayer, uttered in an unfamiliar tongue, that something extraordinary happened to Penelope. She realized that nagging sense of something missing was gone. She wondered why.

Before she could examine this newfound feeling at length, the prayer ended and Sarah nudged her. "Just so you know, the bishop is going to introduce you," she whispered. "Don't be surprised."

"Okay."

Sure enough, after making some announcements in German, the bishop switched to English. "Today I would like to welcome Penelope Moore," he said. "She came in as a guest at Simon Troyer's bed-and-breakfast, but it quickly became apparent that she and Sarah Troyer are identical twins tragically separated at birth. Please make her welcome after the service."

At Sarah's urging, Penelope stood up briefly, nodded and smiled, then dropped back down onto the bench as a buzz of excited conversation rose among the church members who hadn't yet heard the news.

Penelope looked around and saw almost everyone staring at her—and smiling. The overwhelming feeling of both curiosity and acceptance made her blink moisture from her eyes.

She had to resist an overwhelming thought: she had found her home.

After filing out of the barn, Simon stood to the side and watched Penelope become surrounded by well-wishers, greeting her and welcoming her to the community.

Traveling to church with her, it was almost as if he was traveling with a woman he was courting. Or a wife. It was an odd feeling…and a not-unwelcome one.

Could it ever happen? Amish converts were rare. But perhaps Penelope was an exception. She was born to an Amish mother, after all. And her twin was a strong tug.

But he knew better than to get his hopes up…

"Looks like she fits right in, *ja*?" commented his brother Amos, who came to stand beside him.

"*Ja*. I simply can't get over the physical similarities, especially with Penelope in the borrowed dress."

Amos shot him a glance. "She's not Amish," he warned. "Don't get any ideas."

"I'm not." Simon recognized how defensive he sounded. "It's just…"

"It's just that you're lonely and want a wife. I know," Amos said.

Simon detected a note of sympathy in his brother's voice. "*Ja*, maybe you're right," he admitted. "Now that my business is up and running, I suppose it's normal to think ahead."

"Despite the excitement of a long-lost sister, I can't see Penelope being interested in converting," cautioned Amos. "Aside from the usual complications, she wasn't raised in any faith, *ja*? That's a hard thing to overcome."

"I know. Believe me, I know. But even a cat may look at a king." He grinned. "You found Sarah pretty enough to marry. Now I can admire someone who's just as pretty without feeling like I'm crossing any boundaries."

Amos laughed and clapped a hand on Simon's shoulder. "You're right," he agreed. "You've always been a *gut* brother to my wife. Enjoy the view."

Lines started forming at the food tables. *"Komm,"* said Simon. "I assume I can sit with you and Sarah?"

"*Ja* sure. And since Penelope no doubt will be sitting with us too, you'll have the opportunity to…enjoy the scenery some more."

Simon made a face at his brother, then got in line behind him to get some food.

By the time he and Amos were able to join the sisters at the picnic table, Simon found himself on the outskirts of a cluster of older women who were clucking over Penelope.

Penelope caught his eye and managed to convey an eye roll without actually performing the gesture. He grinned at her predicament. He could tell she was enjoying herself. She was even trying out some rudimentary German.

Yes, it was too easy to imagine she was truly a member of the church and not a stranger dressed up in costume. He was going to have to be very careful to keep his budding feelings to himself.

At last the time came for the potluck to conclude. Simon found himself helping to load the benches from the church service onto the special wagon made to hold them. The wagon was normally parked inside the Stoltzfuses' barn between uses, since most of the time they hosted the church services. However, since a few other families were now in the rotation, having the wagons loaded and ready to go was useful.

He walked up to Penelope and Sarah—who was holding little Eleanor on her hip—just in time to hear Sarah say "…next Wednesday?"

"What's on Wednesday?" he asked.

"I was just asking if she wanted to help make raspberry jam at Esther Mast's house," explained Sarah. "There will be a group of us, and Esther has a large stove."

"Will she go in Amish garb?" he couldn't help ask.

"If she wants to, *ja*," retorted Sarah, though she

smiled as she did so. "I told her she could keep the dress and apron as long as she wants."

"The women in this church are so nice!" exclaimed Penelope. "I'm sure it's just because you're my sister, but I don't think I've ever been welcomed as much as I have been here."

"*Ja*, we're a *gut* group of people," agreed Sarah, before raising her voice a bit. "Paul! *Liebling*, it's time to go."

"I'll have the horse hitched up in a few minutes," Simon told Penelope. "If you could gather the lunch hamper and dishes, I'll be ready to pick you up in a few minutes."

"I'll be ready." Penelope gave him a dazzling smile and moved off toward the food tables.

Simon stared after her for the briefest moment. *Off limits*, he reminded himself.

She was ready by the time he pulled the buggy around. When she was aboard, he clucked to the horse and started down the lane.

"What did you think?" he inquired.

"It was…" She paused as if groping for a word. "Amazing," she finally said.

"What was amazing? The church service? The potluck? The little old ladies giving you the third degree?"

"All of the above. I couldn't follow everything being said during the sermon, but I got the gist. I think he was talking about debt, which is something I have personal experience with. I need to ask him what the Bible says about debt."

"Are you in debt?" he asked, surprised.

Her face shuttered. "It's been a rough couple of months,"

she admitted, "and that's all I'll say about it. It's none of your business."

"Of course not." But he was sorry to see the joy drain from her face, so he changed the subject. "So this jam-making party—did Sarah invite you, or someone else?"

"Someone else. I think her name was Abigail. She said they're overflowing with raspberries at the moment, so we'll spend a couple hours picking and then turn them into jam."

"You seem to have a gift for making friends," he remarked. "It's something I struggle with, which seems kind of hard to admit for someone who runs a B&B."

She was silent a moment. "Have you ever thought about coming under a franchise?" she asked in a slightly strangled tone.

He shot her a look. "A franchise? What do you mean? I'm not a fast-food restaurant."

"Well, there are companies that have bed-and-breakfast properties listed in their name. The B&Bs are run according to standardized guidelines. It ensures each establishment is up to an identical standard of quality."

"Why would I want to do that?" he asked, puzzled. "I want to run my business the way I think it should be run."

"Even if there's room for improvement?"

He tried not to be annoyed. "Have you noticed anything I need to improve? Your room? The meals? The location?"

"No, of course not. It's just… Well, it strikes me that it would be, well, easier to run a place if you don't have to be responsible for all the decisions or the marketing or even the advertising."

"Admittedly those *are* areas where I could use some improvement," he noted, "but I'd want to do it on my own terms, not some corporate overlord's ideas."

"Hmm." Penelope averted her face to study the surrounding countryside.

An element of doubt crept into Simon. *Was* there something that needed improvement in his hospitality? He was offering Penelope just the same kind of service that he'd provided to previous customers, to their high praise. The only thing he was doing differently with Penelope was getting a little more personal—introducing her to Sarah, sitting with her at meals. Well, he didn't regret introducing her to her long-lost twin, but if he was getting too personal at mealtimes or even by offering to drive her to church, he would remedy that right away. He didn't want to do anything to make her stay uncomfortable.

"Catch a clue," he muttered to himself. He vowed he would be more watchful for clues of anything that would make her feel awkward.

Chapter Eight

If there was one thing Penelope loved to do, it was to color in a sketch.

Starting with the outline she had earlier sketched in pencil on canvas, she mixed acrylics and began turning the sketch into a living painting. It never failed to amaze her how she was able to bring a scene to life. She knew she had a gift, but where that gift came from was anyone's guess. Neither of her parents had any skills in art. Nor, it seemed, did Sarah.

But she'd always loved art. This interlude at Simon's B&B was, she realized, a guilt-free opportunity to indulge in her favorite passion.

What she'd seen so far of the Amish community—the solemn church service, the conviviality of the potluck afterward, quilting with the women under a shady tree—they all begged to be painted.

At the moment, she was working on the quilting scene. But soon, she wanted to paint something else.

Simon. Simon in the garden below her window, picking peas. She'd watched him the evening before and sketched the scene: a basket at his feet half-full of the pea pods, his body framed by the beds luxuriant with other vegetables such as beans and tomatoes. The straw hat obscured his face, but his suspenders and broadfall trousers were classically Amish.

It was a beautiful scene with a beautiful—well, handsome—man. Penelope couldn't help but record it. Yes, she would paint him in his garden...and then give him the painting.

But that would be in the future. For now, she worked on the quilting scene. She mixed paints and started applying first the foundational parts—the grass and sky. Over these, she would start to create the background: trees, house. Then in the foreground would come the focus of the painting: the quilting frame with the colorful quilt, and the bright garments of the women bent over their stitching...

In the middle of envisioning how the final piece would look, Penelope was startled by the sound of her cell phone ringing. She had hardly looked at her cell phone since arriving in Montana, and with a clutch of guilt she wondered if it was her employer, QuirkyB&B.

But no, it was her mother. "Hi, Mom!" She put her phone on speaker so she could continue to paint.

"Hi, dear. Your dad and I wanted to let you know what we found out about the adoption agency."

Her mother put her own phone on speaker so both parents could join the conversation.

"What did you find out?" Penelope demanded.

Walter, her father, blew out a breath of frustration. "Not as much as we'd like," he admitted. "We found the adoption agency had been involved in a controversial experiment several decades ago in which they split up twins and even a set of triplets for psychological investigations. Some of the adoptive parents of the earlier splits knew about the experiment, but when it came to light what was happening, there was a huge scandal. The agency went underground and reemerged with a different identity, and went about splitting twins much more quietly." He choked slightly. "Your mother and I had no idea you were a twin, honey."

"I know, Dad." Penelope knew he spoke the truth. Her parents would never lie about such a matter, nor would they have agreed to anything as unethical as separating twins. "I assume the agency was shut down when this was discovered?"

"Yes, this time permanently. We haven't been able to find anything specifically about you and your sister, but obviously you were part of that second wave of splits. Has anyone ever contacted you about a psychological profile or anything?"

"No. I'll ask Sarah, but I suspect she'll have the same answer." She sighed. "So it seems we were split up for no reason, not even this so-called research which, I assume, was to measure the whole 'nature versus nurture' question. What a waste."

"We'll keep researching what we can," said her father, "but there doesn't seem to be much by way of information we can find so many years after the fact."

"Don't obsess about it," said Penelope. "What's done is done, and none of us can change the past. Both Sarah and I had good parents and childhoods, so things could have been much worse."

"Tell us what's happening over there in Montana," her mother urged.

So Penelope filled her parents in on the various activities to which she'd been invited, the people she'd met and the art projects she hoped to complete. She also mentioned how she'd dressed in her sister's clothes when she went to the church service, just to tease people. "It's really a wonderful little community I landed in," she concluded. "I'm sure it has to do with my physical similarity to Sarah, but everyone's been so welcoming."

"You sound so much more relaxed," observed her mother. "You were always wound up so tight when you worked for the marketing agency. Now even your voice has changed."

"Has it?" Penelope considered this. "I think you might be right. This whole area just seems designed for a slower lifestyle." She gave a little sigh. "I have to confess, I find myself wishing I wasn't here to try to talk the B&B owner into coming under the Quirky franchise. He's an independent fellow, and I don't think he'll want to. I just wish I could paint."

"Well, nothing says you have to stay at this job forever," her father said. "For that matter, maybe you can look around at the local job market. It would certainly keep you closer to your sister."

"I don't think I can find anything that pays what I'm getting paid now," Penelope replied. "With this credit card bill hanging over my head, my first priority is to pay it off. The town of Pierce is so small, I can't imagine a lot of people are earning more than minimum wage."

She talked with her parents for a few more minutes, then said goodbye. She looked around the pretty little room and indulged in a brief fantasy about what it would be like to stay. At the moment, however, she didn't see how that would work.

From below, she heard voices. She recognized Simon,

but no one else. Curious, she opened her door and listened.

Visitors. It seemed the guests Simon had been expecting were now here, and he was checking them in. Leaving her door open, she returned to her painting, hoping to catch a glimpse of the newcomers as they were shown to their room.

For the first time she wondered what it was like to run a B&B. It seemed like a prime opportunity to meet people from every walk of life. Penelope knew Simon had the gift of hospitality, of making strangers feel at home. He certainly had done that with her. How would he behave with these new guests? Her interest was piqued.

Within a few minutes, the voices grew louder as they ascended the stairs. Through the open door, she saw Simon carrying luggage, followed by an older couple.

Simon paused. "This is a guest already staying here," he said to the couple. "Penelope Moore, this is Arthur and Beth Tresedor."

"How do you do?" greeted Penelope. She hastily wiped down with a rag and held out her hand. "I'm sorry, I was painting."

"Oh, are you an artist?" inquired Arthur Tresedor.

"Yes. Just taking a few weeks to concentrate on capturing this part of the world."

"We'd love to see your work sometime," said Beth Tresedor. She smiled politely and followed Simon down the hall.

Penelope watched as the couple chattered between themselves. They seemed like pleasant people, but unquestionably their very presence changed the private, almost intimate, feeling of the B&B. She was no longer alone with Simon; she shared the space with the other couple. She shrugged—what else could she expect?—and returned to her painting.

An hour later she took a break and went downstairs, hoping to snag a cup of tea.

"Guten tag," Simon greeted her as she entered the kitchen. He was engaged in chopping vegetables. "Just so you know, the Tresedors have opted to have dinners as well as breakfast, so you'll have company in the dining room."

"I don't mind," Penelope lied gallantly. She realized how much she looked forward to talking with Simon privately. "You have to make a living, after all."

"Ja, and these are the best kind of guests. They're appreciative and not complainers."

"Are these the overnight stay you mentioned, or the week-longers?"

"The overnighters. They're traveling to Washington State tomorrow."

"I see." Unasked, Penelope started a kettle and pulled a large ceramic mug from a cabinet. "By the way, my parents called a while ago to tell me what they learned about the adoption agency. Short answer, not much." She repeated the conversation.

Simon shook his head. "I know for a fact Sarah's parents feel the same as yours—that had they known Sarah was a twin, they wouldn't have hesitated to raise you both. They're *gut* people."

"I almost can't find it in myself to waste any energy on anger," Penelope admitted. "I just feel sorry for the other pairs who were split up who won't have the chance to meet their twin."

"The feeling that something is missing—do you still have it?"

Penelope poured hot water over a tea bag. "Yes," she admitted. "I don't know where it comes from." She gave an awkward chuckle. "Oddly, when I was listening to the hymn singing at church, I noticed it was gone. I'm so used to feeling this low background feeling that its absence was noticeable. I don't know why."

"I have an idea about that, but I don't know if you're ready to hear it."

"An idea about what? The cause of this feeling something is missing?"

"Ja." Simon scraped chopped carrots and potatoes into a pot. "You said meeting Sarah didn't change that feeling. But listening to hymns did. I wonder if you're feeling a lack of faith in *Gott*?"

Had Simon started tap-dancing across the kitchen, Penelope couldn't have been more surprised. "Faith?" she repeated.

To Simon, it was obvious Penelope was a searching soul. But the moment he stated as much, he could have kicked himself.

The Amish were not evangelizers. In general, faith was something most people were reluctant to vocalize about, much less discuss with others. They preferred a quiet witness.

But it hurt to see Penelope floundering around when it was clear to him what the problem was. Still, he wouldn't push. He *couldn't* push.

"Forget I said that," he prevaricated. "It's none of my business."

She frowned and stared at her mug as she dipped the tea bag up and down. After a few moments she said, "I guess I wouldn't know. How does someone feel a *lack* of something?"

"I shouldn't have said what I said," he repeated. With some relief, he heard the Tresedors coming down the stairs.

"I probably should not be caught in the kitchen," she quipped, picking up her mug. "I'll go back up to my room and work on my painting."

"Ja gut," he replied. "Dinner is at six o'clock."

He watched her through the service window as she passed the Tresedors, nodding politely, and climbed the stairs. He felt flustered by his growing interest in what, after all, was nothing more than a paying guest.

Except…she wasn't just a paying guest anymore. Technically she was a relative, the sister of his sister-in-law.

In fact, now that she was a relation of sorts, he realized he was seeing her differently. Despite the physical similarities, Penelope was *not* Sarah. She was more confident, more worldly, more exuberant than her more sedate twin. He enjoyed seeing the sparkle of interest in her eyes when encountering something new, such as quilting or singing hymns or even the backyard chicken coop.

But Sarah had something Penelope lacked: a sureness of her station in life. Sarah was a respected member of the community, a loving wife and mother, an upright woman within the church. By contrast, Penelope was a wanderer. She admitted she moved from place to place for her art, never settling down.

Yes, there were too many obstacles between them, starting with what he'd just pointed out: her lack of faith.

His beliefs weren't just a cloak he donned for Sunday church and then removed for the rest of the week. They were an integral part of his being, a constant and comforting presence he could never put aside. And Penelope, as intriguing as she was, did not share that faith. He knew he had to keep his distance.

Fortunately the new guests provided the distraction he needed.

"Of course you can see the garden," he said in response to their request. "Would you like a tour?"

The Tresedors were warm and interesting people, full of questions and praise in equal measure. Simon answered the usual queries about the Amish church. He told them about the modest attractions in the nearby town of Pierce. He inquired politely about their travel plans and where they lived. In short, he developed a superficial friendship with his guests, something for which he had a knack.

And when he told them dinner would be served shortly and steered them back to the dining room, he was surprised to see Penelope already seated at a table, a sketch pad in front of her.

Simon peeled off and returned to his meal preparation in the kitchen, but watched and listened through the service window as the older couple cooed over Penelope's sketch. Soon they seated themselves at her table, and he heard animated conversation between the two parties.

He grinned. Penelope had even more of a knack for making friends than he did, it seemed.

"Dinner is ready," he called through the window. "Would you like separate tables, or one table?"

"Are we disturbing you?" inquired Arthur Tresedor of Penelope.

"Not at all!" she exclaimed. "You're welcome to have dinner with me."

So Simon found himself serving dinner to all three of his guests sharing the same table, listening to their chatter about places he had never seen and cultural events he had never experienced. Yet he wasn't jealous; he was fascinated.

Penelope's face was animated as she laughed and talked with the guests. Her dark eyes sparkled and she had a slight flush on her cheeks. Though he found his sister-in-law to be a pretty woman, somehow he found Penelope to be nothing short of beautiful.

In some respects, he was glad she was dressed once again in her *Englisch* clothes. It emphasized the differences between them and reminded him why he needed to keep his distance.

But as he had recently remarked to his brother, even a cat could look at a king. Simon knew only too well the boundaries that lay between them…but it didn't prevent him from silently admiring her from a distance.

At last the older couple excused themselves, thanked him for a delicious dinner and trailed upstairs.

"You've made some friends," Simon remarked as he loaded dishes and cutlery onto a tray.

"They're nice people." She gathered her own dishes and stood up to follow him into the kitchen. Unasked, she scraped her plate into the compost bucket and rinsed it. "Did you know Beth Tresedor used to teach literature in a high school? And Arthur said he fancied himself a painter when he was younger, but never did anything with it."

"Huh. I never thought to ask them what their hobbies or occupations are. What are you doing?" he added as she ran hot water into the washbasin and added soap.

She paused. "Oh. I'm so used to doing dishes at my place I never thought I was overstepping my boundaries. Sorry."

He chuckled. "You're a paying guest. There's no reason for you to wash dishes."

"What if I dry?"

"Really, that's not necessary. I let the dishes air dry."

"Then what if I just sit and watch?"

Surprised, he looked at her. She truly seemed interested in staying. Both his hospitality instinct and his personal instinct told him not to argue. "Why don't you make some tea, then?"

"Okay." Comfortable in the kitchen, she heated water and pulled out a tea bag.

"You seem to have a talent for making friends," he observed as he plunged his hands into the hot soapy water. "Even though I run a B&B, it's more difficult for me to chat up strangers."

She spooned a bit of sugar into a mug. "My mother is like that. I'm actually an introvert, but my mom can make anyone feel comfortable. During my awkward teenage years, I remember watching her and making mental notes. I can pull her training out of my pocket when necessary, but I'm also happy spending hours on my own, painting or reading or whatever."

"I'm also introverted." He rinsed a plate and stacked it in the drain rack. "Most of us in the church are, really. It takes work to step outside our comfort zone sometimes, especially among the *Englisch*."

"I didn't get that impression after the church service on Sunday. I don't think I've ever seen a group dive into socializing with such enthusiasm. I didn't see anyone left out."

"That's because we all know each other. When I first arrived here, it took me a little while to relax. Now, it seems every church service is a gathering of my best friends."

"Maybe that's what I felt," she mused. "I mean, there were all these combined kilowatts of faith during the service, but somehow it seemed more than that. There was...I don't know, maybe *love* is the right word... among everyone there."

Simon scrubbed at a stubborn spot on a pot. "That's a *gut* observation," he said. "We're a strong community. Our bishop, he keeps an eagle eye for any potential conflict and does everything he can to diffuse it. It's important to keep any infighting from getting a foothold. But still," he added, giving her a lopsided grin, "I like my quiet time. I have no doubts I'm an introvert."

"Yet you run a B&B." It was a statement, not a question.

"*Ja.* I enjoy hospitality. I learned that early on. It seems like a contradiction, but there you go. I can be a gracious host, but I don't have the gift of conversation with strangers like you do."

"Or like my mother does. I just benefitted from her training." She chuckled. "Between us, we make a good team."

He was startled. A team of what? Hosts? Business partners?

She sipped her tea and seemed content to simply sit and look around the kitchen, but he found his mind abuzz with an unexpected realization: her strengths were his weaknesses. She was at ease with guests and knew her way around computers and advertising and marketing. What a pity he couldn't partner with her to improve his business.

He glanced at her unobtrusively. It was like seeing Sarah without a *kapp* and in *Englisch* clothes, yet already it seemed he could distinguish her from her sister. He preferred her vivaciousness to Sarah's more demure personality.

Stop it, Simon, he warned himself. He resumed his task.

"How difficult is it to live in your place of business?" she inquired, taking a sip of tea. "I mean, I was rude enough a couple days ago when I walked in on you glazing your window to ask about seeing the garden. I imagine that happens a lot. Does the lack of privacy bother you?"

"*Nein*, not really. It will be better when I'm finished renovating it. Then I'll be putting a self-locking door between the two sides of the house for a bit of extra privacy."

"How long before your side of the house is completed?"

"My private quarters, you mean?" He rinsed the pot. "Depends on how much time I put into it. If I had no distractions, I could probably get it done inside a couple months, but of course I have guests and the garden to attend to, not to mention any church-related activities. We have at least one building party a month, sometimes more, since we're still getting infrastructure built for people moving out here from back east."

"Building party?" She perked up. "Like barn raisings and such?"

"*Ja.* Could be a barn, could be a house, could even be something smaller like a coop or shed, though those are just a few men rather than an all-hands activity."

"I'd love to see one of those!"

"Well, you'll have your chance weekend after next, if you want. On Friday and Saturday, we're building a barn for some people on the other side of the settlement. I'm sure Sarah would love to have you helping the women."

"Yes, that would be wonderful! I might bring my sketch pad."

"Well, barn raisings tend to be busy from start to finish," he warned. "It's a big task, getting something built in a day, although the women usually have some time off in the afternoon. You might find yourself quilting again."

"I enjoyed quilting. I admit, I found myself sketching some quilting pattern ideas. I planned to show them to Sarah to see if they could be translated into fabric."

"She would know. Sarah makes wonderful quilts."

She gave a sigh. "You know what, Simon? I like it here. I find myself wishing I could stay."

He suppressed a frisson of delight at the idea. "Well, you're a wandering artist, aren't you? What prevents you from staying as long as you want?"

As before, he watched an almost literal shutter drop over her face. Her expression went from dreamy to troubled. "I… I can't."

He wanted to ask why, but her expression discouraged it. Instead he said, "Well, if you change your mind, you're always welcome to stay on here. Or I'm sure Sarah would love to have you stay with them for a bit."

He was relieved to see her relax. "Yes. Oh, Simon, you have no idea how nice it is to feel *welcomed*. Why do I feel so at home here?"

He had no idea what she meant by that comment, but it pleased him to see her settling in so well.

"I don't know," he replied, "but I'm sure a lot has to do with Sarah."

"And you." The words were blurted, and she made a gesture as if to snatch them back.

But he was pleased. It seemed she was warming up to him as more than just a host.

Stop it, he reprimanded himself again. *That's a fool's game.*

Penelope was staring at her teacup. "I've also been thinking about what you said earlier—that the sense of emptiness I've always felt might have to do with a lack of faith. I don't quite know what to make of it."

Having never felt that lack, Simon didn't know what to say. Instead, he delegated responsibility. "You might consider having a talk with our bishop," he suggested. "He's a *gut* man and might be able to offer some advice."

She looked faintly surprised. "I might do that…"

Simon tried hard not to clutch at a wild hope—that Penelope might someday be baptized Amish so he could court her. It was far too soon in their acquaintance to entertain such thoughts.

But he himself couldn't shake the almost eerie feeling that his future wife was sitting right here in the kitchen with him.

Chapter Nine

Penelope almost forgot she was in Montana for business. Instead, over the next few weeks, she immersed herself so thoroughly in the Amish community that she found herself dreading her departure more and more.

While on the surface she wanted to attribute this to Sarah, the truth was she was looking at Simon as something more than a host. She had spent enough time among other church members to understand the barrier between them—as a baptized man, he could hardly express any romantic interest in her—but that didn't keep her from seeking out his company.

On the day of the barn raising—something she was tremendously looking forward to—she received an early-morning phone call from her boss, Frank, at QuirkyB&B, taking advantage of the time difference between Massachusetts and Montana. He sounded testy at her lack of communication.

"But this facility is off-grid," she reminded him. "I have to go into town to check email because there's no internet connection. I'm surprised I can make phone calls at all."

"Whatever." Frank sounded like he was trying to control his temper. "I knew I should have made you get a smart phone so I could text you. What have you learned so far?"

"That this facility is surprisingly well-run. The manager knows what he's doing."

"But what about its online presence? That's what brought it to our attention in the first place. Looks like a first-grader designed the website."

"That's because it's an Amish-run business. I didn't know that going in."

"Amish!" Frank's voice took on a note of excitement. "I didn't know that, either. That's a great selling point and would be a fantastic addition to our B&B lineup. I hope you're doing your best to convince the owner that joining us would be in his best interest."

"I'm trying, but it's not easy," she warned. "He's not overly motivated by profit."

"Then *make* him motivated," snapped Frank. "Come on, Penelope, your commission is on the line here, and this is your first assignment. I expected better."

Penelope swallowed down hot anger at the implication she was slacking. "I'll do my best, Frank, but if he can't be convinced, he can't be convinced. It's not like I can force him."

"There are ways," her boss concluded in an ominous tone. "Just remember, we're not paying you to take an extended vacation. Keep that in mind." He hung up.

She stared at her flip phone in annoyance, then turned it off to save the battery.

Frank's attitude had shown her a dark side of QuirkyB&B, and she wasn't sure she liked it. It was one thing to be taught aggressive pressure tactics during training; it was another to put those tactics into practice in a real-world situation—especially with a man for whom she was developing some extremely strong feelings.

Okay, if she were honest with herself, her feelings for Simon were getting deeper. A lot deeper. In fact, she was in serious danger of falling in love with the man, which would mess up her plans in a big way.

But Frank was right about one thing: her commission was on the line. If Simon refused to join QuirkyB&B, her paycheck would amount to little more than minimum wage, nowhere near enough to pay off her credit card bill. She also couldn't forget QuirkyB&B was supposed to reimburse her for her stay here.

Besides, her conscience pricked a little. She *had* been enjoying herself too much on company time. It was just so easy to get wrapped up in her new situation…

She sighed and dropped into the rocking chair in her room, looking at the art pieces she'd finished so far. The quilting bee was her first one, and she liked the result— bright colors, peaceful setting. She'd finished another piece as well, depicting the vegetable garden, with a glimpse of the fenced chicken yard to one side. Her next piece was still on the easel, and showed a scene during the potluck after the church service she had attended.

Painting these scenes etched them in her mind. Even planning to paint a scene forced her to note details she might otherwise have missed.

As she looked at the unfinished piece on the easel, she experienced a moment of depression. She loved painting, but who would ever buy her work? She was a complete unknown in the competitive art world. No one would ever give her money for her skills. She had never actually sold anything. All her earlier artwork had been given away to friends. There was no way she could ever pay off that bill through painting.

She sighed, picked up her sketchbook and walked downstairs.

"All ready to go?" inquired Simon. He had a tool belt slung over one shoulder and carried a wooden toolbox.

"Yes," she replied. "It's nice of Sarah and Amos to drive us to the work site."

"*Ja*. It's because Amos has a wagon. I don't."

Simon locked the door behind them, and she fell into place next to him as they made their way to her sister's home. She wondered what she needed to do to convince Simon to come under the QuirkyB&B umbrella.

"I've been thinking about your marketing," she finally blurted. "And I wonder if you wouldn't be better off turning the whole thing over to experts."

"*Ja*, probably," he said, unfazed. "I've thought about hiring someone in town."

"Actually, I mean some experts who run B&Bs. There are national marketing groups which specialize in advertising those kinds of businesses. It might be financially worthwhile exploring that kind of option."

Simon frowned. "I'm just getting started. I can't afford to hire a big company like that."

"That's the thing, you wouldn't have to. They would do the marketing and advertising for you."

"*Ja*, sure they would." His words just barely bordered on sarcastic, a tone she'd never heard him use. "But what's the catch?"

"They might be able to broaden your exposure in exchange for a share of the profits." There, she'd said it.

"Then I'm not interested," replied Simon. "If I'm going to hire someone to help me with marketing and advertising, I'd rather just pay them a set fee and be done with it. Besides, having a big company try to run my business would take away the whole purpose behind running a business—the satisfaction of making it succeed through my own work."

Penelope sighed to herself. It was what she'd expected. Simon's independence was a formidable barrier to her goal…and, if she was truthful, it was an aspect of his character she admired.

"Well, it still could be something you might consider," she said, as they approached Sarah's house. "Having corporate backing almost guarantees your B&B will always be full. Look, there's Amos." She changed the subject almost desperately.

Amos raised an arm in greeting as he continued placing tools in the back of the wagon. *"Guder mariye!"* he called.

"Guder mariye," Simon replied. He glanced at Penelope. "I'll help Amos pack the rest of the tools we'll need. You might see if Sarah needs any help."

"Okay." She got the distinct impression he was annoyed at her, and could she blame him? Even the slight censure made her uneasy, and she realized how much she valued his good opinion.

Inside the house, Sarah's kitchen was a place of domestic chaos. Little Eleanor toddled around the kitchen clutching a wooden spoon, which she used to drum on various things.

"Guder mariye," her sister said cheerfully. "Your first barn raising! Are you excited?"

"Yes, actually I am. You're bringing all this food?" she added in surprise.

"Ja," Sarah replied, placing another container inside the enormous wicker hamper. "The men, they work so hard. They're very, very hungry by the time lunch rolls around. You'd be surprised how quickly this will all disappear. *Nein, liebling,* ask your aunt Penelope," she added to Paul, who wanted help tucking his shirt into his trousers.

Pleased the child was becoming more comfortable with her, Penelope knelt in front of the boy and assisted him in adjusting his clothing. "There!" she concluded brightly, tousling his fair hair. "Now you look as handsome as your father."

The boy giggled, and Sarah smiled at her son. "Go see if *Daed* needs help with the wagon," she told him in German.

"Ja, Mamm." Paul darted outside.

"He's adorable." Penelope rose to her feet. "Both your kids are."

"Danke." A beatific smile wreathed Sarah's face. "I love being a *mamm.*"

"Sometimes I wonder if I ever will be." Penelope didn't mean for her comment to hold such pathos.

Sarah glanced at her sharply. "You're only twenty-eight. There's time."

"I know. It's just that…" Penelope made a gesture of frustration. "I don't seem to be *getting* anywhere in life, you know? It's like I'm marking time."

"Don't fret," her sister advised. "You have no idea what *Gott* has in store."

Amos entered the kitchen. "Ready, *lieb*?" he asked. "The wagon is packed."

"*Ja*, sure. Penelope, can you carry the diaper bag?"

"Of course." She seized the cloth bag while Sarah picked up the toddler and Amos hefted the food hamper into his arms.

The combined parties made for a full wagon. Penelope sat in back with Simon and little Paul, while Sarah perched Eleanor in her lap and Amos drove. Nestled among the toolboxes and tool belts, she watched as Amos clucked to the horse and the wagon started down the road with a small jolt.

"It looks like others are heading there, too," she remarked to Simon, pointing at other wagons pulling onto the road. She heard snatches of song.

"*Ja*, this is an all-hands-on-deck work party," he replied, pulling his nephew onto his lap. "It's a new family that moved in from Ohio over the summer. They need a barn before the snow flies since he's a dairy farmer. We'll get the basic structure up today, and tomorrow we might even be able to get some of the interior done, such as calf pens and a milking parlor, but the family will have a lot of finish work to do themselves afterward."

"This is something I admire so much." She watched as yet another wagon pulled out of a driveway and onto the road, joining the throng heading for the destination farm. "The cooperation that makes everyone's lives easier."

"It's the best force-multiplier there is," Simon agreed. "Remember what I said about how individualism is subsumed for the good of the community? This is how it works."

Penelope was suddenly ashamed of herself for her role in pushing Simon toward QuirkyB&B. It was clear his motivation was to make the business succeed on his own terms, for whatever reason. To take that satisfaction away from him seemed heartless.

She had a lot to learn from Simon, and from Sarah, and from the church community as a whole. His B&B was not meant to be part of a corporate chain, but rather an individual contribution toward a community whole. Who was she to pressure him to diminish that contribution?

And yet...

And yet that credit card bill, sitting on her bedside table, was a constant reminder of her purpose here. After her parents' experience while growing up, being in debt terrified her.

What should she do?

And then she did something she never thought to do: she prayed about it. *God, what should I do?*

When Amos pulled the horse to a halt at the barn site, Simon shouldered his tool belt and grabbed two toolboxes. "I'll get everything off-loaded," he told his brother, "then you can go unhitch the horse."

"Ja, gut," Amos replied.

Penelope climbed down from the wagon and held up her arms for Paul. "Come, little one," she told him. "Your mom can tell you where you can and can't go, okay?"

Amos held little Eleanor while Sarah climbed down from the wagon, then handed down the baby. In a few moments, Simon had the wagon emptied. "You'll be okay?" he asked Penelope.

"Of course," she replied, dazzling him with an eager smile. "I have Sarah to show me the ropes."

He nodded, grabbed his tools and headed for the work site.

It seemed the whole church was here. He stood for a few minutes, trying to see the scene through a stranger's eyes.

Men milled about, donning tool belts and gathering around Adam Chupp, whom Simon knew usually acted as foreman on these projects. An *Englisch youngie* named Jeremy, one of Adam's employees, stood with the other men, listening intently. A few of the older men rounded up the younger boys. The youngsters would be set toward some of the simpler carpentry tasks—hammering nails, measuring lumber.

The girls—those who weren't running around and playing—helped the women set up food on the tables, along with coolers of homemade lemonade. Simon grinned. Lemonade was, in his mind, forever associated with community construction projects. He loved the stuff.

His eyes were drawn, invariably, toward Penelope's trim figure, outfitted in an *Englisch* skirt and blouse and sticking close to Sarah. But she looked like she was having a *gut* time—laughing and chattering with the women, helping to spread the food out on the tables.

"Simon!" called Adam Chupp. "Are you working today?"

"*Ja*, of course." He strode toward the men who were being divided into teams. Amos caught his eye and raised a single eyebrow, silently questioning his tardiness. Simon gave a half shrug, hoping his brother wouldn't tease or say anything about his interest in Penelope. His older brother had already guessed too closely about Simon's thoughts regarding his guest.

Simon listened carefully to Adam's directions and his assigned duties. He found himself paired with his brother, working on a truss.

"You might want to be careful," Amos warned. "Watching Penelope the way you do."

Fortunately the sound of hammering and men talking made his brother's words inaudible to anyone else. Simon scowled. "Is it so obvious?"

"Maybe it's just me, but *ja*, it seems obvious. It won't work, Simon. You have to understand that."

Simon banged vigorously on a nail. "What the head says and what the heart says are sometimes two different things."

"Well, you'd better listen to your head, little *bruder*," said Amos, "unless you want to find yourself shunned."

"Don't worry, I'm not doing anything that would get me shunned." Simon snapped out his tape measure, marked a board, then started sawing it to size. "But is it such a bad thing to try to sway her toward the church?"

"*Ja*, maybe. Not because she wouldn't be a welcome member, but because she's *Englisch*, and you know what the bishop always says about the chances of *Englisch* conversions. They're not likely to stick."

Simon knew his brother spoke the truth. So, for that matter, did the bishop. But still, he saw nothing wrong with trying to guide Penelope toward something she clearly lacked.

"I promise not to do anything that would jeopardize my standing in the church," he said stubbornly, "but neither will I try to discourage her from any interest she shows. She was born to an Amish mother, and her twin sister is Amish. Is it so unlikely that she would be curious about her roots?"

Amos glanced over toward the groups of women, and Simon followed his gaze. Penelope was easy to spot in her *Englisch* clothing. She looked animated and happy, chatting with Eva Hostetler and holding little Eleanor in her arms.

"Well, don't say I didn't warn you," Amos said. "Me personally, I understand why you're pulled toward her. It's probably the same instinct that pulled me toward Sarah. All I'm saying is she's off-limits as long as she isn't a member of the church."

"Believe me, Amos, no one knows that better than I do." Simon's defensiveness drained away. He knew his older brother's warnings stemmed from genuine concern about what could happen if Simon courted an unbaptized woman. "All I'm saying is I feel she could be the one."

"Mighty big words for someone you've known for such a short time."

"*Ja*, but I've known Sarah my whole life. Penelope is just a more interesting version." He grinned and ducked as Amos chucked a small piece of wood at him.

The work continued steadily through lunch. Simon didn't think it unusual when Penelope was the one who brought lemonade to both him and Amos.

"Did they assign us to you?" inquired Simon, gulping the cold liquid and wiping his brow with a handkerchief.

"Yes," she replied with candor. "Sarah thought it

would be better if I helped out the men I already knew, rather than bring drinks to strangers."

"That sounds like my Sarah." Amos grinned and drained his glass. "*Danke*, Penelope."

"I'll be back in about fifteen minutes," she replied. "That's how frequently Sarah says you need something to drink."

"She's not wrong. *Danke*," Simon added, handing her his empty glass.

Simon made sure not to watch as she walked away. Amos might be the most observant, but Simon didn't want anyone else to jump to conclusions.

But his brother's warnings set his mind on another path. Was it possible for Penelope to join the church? She had ties beyond those of most *Englischers*. He found himself troubled, and thought it might be best to bring his concerns to the bishop. The church leader was a wise man, and a discreet one. Simon knew his conversations would stay confidential.

He glanced over to where the graybeards sat under the shade of some large pine trees. Often these men undertook to instruct the younger boys during such community projects, but today there were so many people that the older men felt no compunction about sitting this one out. Simon grinned to himself. He remembered his own grandfather enjoying that privilege.

Yes, he would ask for an appointment with the bishop.

His opportunity came late in the afternoon. Simon went to fetch a box of nails from the pile of inventory materials under a nearby tree. As he returned, he saw Samuel Beiler carrying a fresh plate of cookies, obviously with the intention of sharing them among the other men with whom he was sitting.

Simon made sure his trajectory intersected the older man's path. "*Guder mariye*, Bishop," said Simon. "I wonder if you have a moment?"

"*Ja* sure," Samuel Beiler replied, pausing on the path. "Is something troubling you?"

"Perhaps. I was hoping to make an appointment to speak to you. No hurry, it's nothing urgent, just a concern I have."

The older man's eyes sharpened, and Simon had the uneasy feeling the bishop already knew what the discussion would entail.

"Next week, perhaps? I'm free most of Wednesday."

"*Ja* sure. *Danke*, Bishop." Simon nodded his thanks and headed back to the work site.

The bishop was a fair man. Simon could anticipate the church leader repeating Amos's warnings, but what Simon wanted to know was how he might sway Penelope into exploring the possibility of becoming Amish.

When he returned to his duties, Amos collared him. "What did you say to the bishop?"

"I just took your advice and asked for a counseling session," Simon replied. "I figure it can't hurt to lay my burden before him. Samuel's a wise man. If anyone is capable of guiding Penelope into the church, he is. Or, alternately, he could easily warn me to drop the issue entirely. Either way, I'd rather lay it on the line, especially since I can trust in him keeping the issue confidential. As I expect you to do, too." He glared at Amos.

His older brother chuckled. "You have my word. And believe it or not, I'm rooting for you. I like Penelope, and I know it would mean the world to Sarah if her new-found twin was here to stay. I don't think I've ever seen my wife as happy as the last couple of weeks. Those two complement each other so well, it makes me all mushy inside." He made a comical face.

Simon laughed out loud, his good humor restored. "Well, then, I expect you to pray about it," he retorted with a grin. "It's a big project we're asking *Gott* to do, but we can move mountains with the right amount of faith."

"Should I mention this to Sarah or keep it to myself?" inquired Amos with more seriousness.

"Keep it to yourself," replied Simon. "I don't want to get her hopes up."

"Especially in her condition." Amos glanced at him sideways.

"Her condi— Ah, congratulations, big *bruder*." Simon reached over and shook his brother's hand.

"Danke."

He returned to his hammering, trying not to feel jealous of Amos's marital happiness. Was he pinning his hopes where no hope existed? He didn't know. All he could do, he realized, was lay the matter at *Gott*'s feet.

But a little help from the bishop would be welcome as well.

Chapter Ten

After two days of helping with the barn raising, Penelope felt very accepted by the other women in the church community. She was even starting to make conversation in her schoolgirl German, and was picking up more and more of the chatter around her.

On Sunday morning, dressed once again in attire borrowed from Sarah, she admitted to herself how much she was looking forward to the church service. She just hoped the bishop's sermon wouldn't involve the evils of being in debt this time. She glanced at the credit card bill on her bedside table and grimaced.

Besides, perhaps the church atmosphere would give her a better opportunity to ask God for guidance about her job. If she was to sacrifice her QuirkyB&B commission by not pressuring Simon to be franchised, it would mean two things. One, she wouldn't be able to pay off her debt. And two, she would no longer have an excuse to linger in the community. If her job here was done, she would be assigned another commissioned project elsewhere. And who knew where it might be? The only certainty was she would leave the area.

And she didn't want to leave.

She had a sister now, and Penelope couldn't imagine giving her up now that she'd met her. But, if she was honest with herself, Simon was as big a pull as Sarah. She admired his quiet strength and efficiency, so different than the success-driven men she'd met in the workforce. Those men had fancy degrees behind their names, wore power suits to the office and acted as if climbing the corporate ladder was the only thing worth doing.

By contrast, Simon had single-handedly created an oasis of calm on his three acres. He grew a dazzling garden, cultivated a flock of friendly chickens, created meals of delectable taste from local ingredients and otherwise proved himself every bit as successful in his own way as her power-hungry colleagues from her Boston advertising job had been.

Yes, the contrast between her old life and this new—if temporary—existence was enormous. She couldn't help but feel she wanted to stay.

"Then maybe you should talk to our bishop," Simon advised when she confessed this to him on the drive to church. "I'm sure he'll have some advice he can offer."

"Yes, I might do that. He seems like a nice man."

"He is. Church leaders are chosen by lot, since that process reveals *Gott*'s will in the matter. In this case it's clear he was the right man for the job."

"Seems kind of random. Have you ever had the wrong man for the job?"

"None that I've known, though I suppose it's possible. But in the *Englisch* world, there are lots of people who shouldn't be pastors, so there's that."

Penelope knew what to expect at the church service

now, and received many more smiles this time. In fact, she was able to greet quite a number of women by name.

She sat with Sarah, and was pleased when little Eleanor consented to sit on her lap for a few minutes. "She's at the age where she only wants her *mamm* or *daed*," said Sarah, "but I think she feels drawn to you because of our physical similarities."

"She's darling." Penelope wrapped her arms around the toddler and wondered if she would ever have one of her own.

The service began, and Penelope was able to start picking out tunes and even some of the German lyrics. Beside her, Sarah sang in a decent contralto voice, confident with the music she had known since infancy. Penelope felt a mild sting of envy at her sister's solid place in the church.

Her growing ease with the language meant she was able to follow the gist of the sermon. And the gist sent her into a tailspin of confusion.

The bishop kept using the term "called"—*gerufen*—and she wasn't sure she understood what he meant. Called? Did God *call* people? How could that even happen?

The thought occupied her mind through the remainder of the church service. It made her more determined to talk with the bishop.

She had her opportunity as the after-service potluck was winding down. Penelope sat with Sarah, Amos and Simon, and she watched with lively interest as children—including little Paul—darted around, playing and laughing. Eleanor was too sleepy for such games and rested on her mother's shoulder, her eyelids heavy.

The bishop strolled up, clearly making the rounds to chat with people.

"Guten tag," he greeted.

"Guten tag," said Simon and Amos simultaneously. Simon added, "Beautiful day."

"Ja. Penelope, how are you settling in?" inquired the older man, his eyes twinkling.

Penelope touched her *kapp.* "I still feel a bit like I'm playing dress-up, but I have to admit it makes me feel more comfortable when I attend a church service. And more respectful than wearing my regular clothes, too."

"You certainly look like you fit right in."

She knew this was her opportunity. "Everyone has been so welcoming. Which reminds me… Mr. Beiler, do you take appointments to talk with people? I have a few questions I wouldn't mind asking."

The church leader's bushy eyebrows rose slightly. "Of course. I had something tomorrow that got canceled. Would the afternoon do?"

"Thank you. That would be fine."

He nodded. "Simon can instruct you how to find my house." He strolled off, stopping to speak with some other church members.

"What kinds of questions did you want to ask?" inquired Sarah, shifting her toddler to the other shoulder.

It was too soon to admit to curiosity about the term *called* that caught her attention—she needed to think it over some more—but she was honest about her other feelings.

"I feel pulled to stay longer here," she admitted. She smiled at her sister. "You're a part of that feeling, of course, but it's more than that. I don't think I've ever felt so at home or welcomed as I have here. I… I guess what I want to talk to him about is whether it's possible to stay longer." There, she'd said it.

Sarah's eyes sparkled. "That would be wonderful!"

Penelope saw Amos give a lightning glance at his brother, then smiled at her. "*Ja*, that would be wonderful," he echoed.

"Yes, well, we'll see." Penelope stared at her plate, wishing at the moment she'd never even heard of QuirkyB&B. "I just don't know if it will work out."

"Why wouldn't it?" inquired Sarah. "You're an artist. Your time and schedule are your own, aren't they?"

How could she even admit she'd never even sold a single painting? "It's…it's a little more complicated than that," she prevaricated. It was not, she now knew, the Amish way to probe, and was relieved when Simon changed the subject and started talking with Amos about shoeing horses.

Later, while the men hitched up horses and gathered the benches used during the church service, Sarah and Penelope began collecting dishes and packing them in hampers.

"If you do decide to stay longer," Sarah told Penelope in a low voice, "we have room in our house. Amos already agreed you could stay in one of our spare bedrooms. That way you wouldn't have to keep paying Simon to stay in the B&B. I just wanted to let you know."

"Oh, Sarah…" Penelope leaned over and hugged her sister. "That means more to me than I can say."

"I'm just being selfish," Sarah replied, her eyes suspiciously bright. "It's not every day I have a twin sister come out of the woodwork, *ja*? It's selfish of me to want to keep you nearby."

"That makes two of us." Penelope sighed. "But as I said earlier, it's a bit more complicated than that."

"What's making it complicated?"

Not for anything could Penelope confess her deception or motives for staying at Simon's B&B. Instead, she decided on a partial truth. "I'm in some debt," she admitted. "For the last two months I was in Boston, I was low on cash and had to put the rent on my credit card. Then when my rent skyrocketed, I couldn't afford to live in Boston any longer. So here I am, roaming around the country but with a huge credit card bill hanging over my head."

"Oh my." Sarah looked concerned. "If I may ask, how big?"

"Over seven thousand dollars."

Sarah went pale. "Seven thousand dollars!" she gasped. "For two months' worth of rent?"

"Yes. Now you know why I couldn't afford to stay there any longer."

"You'd have to sell a lot of paintings each month just to pay for a place to live!"

"It was always a struggle." Even with her marketing job, paying rent was a challenge. "By comparison, Simon's B&B is far less expensive."

"Well, if you decide to stay with us, your rent will be nothing," said Sarah stoutly.

Penelope's eyes stung. "And if that's the case, you can bet I'll be doing everything I can to make your burden easier," she replied. "I don't want to be a freeloader."

"You're family."

The simple words went straight to Penelope's heart. "Family," she sighed. "For my whole life, the only family I had was my parents. Now I have you and Amos and the children."

"Sounds to me like you've come home," Sarah observed.

Penelope was startled. Could that be true?

"It's Sunday," observed Simon later that afternoon, sitting in the rocking chair on the front porch and sipping a glass of lemonade. "It's a day of rest, but to be honest I often find my work more restful than my rest, especially when it comes to the garden."

"The view from this porch is so pretty that I'm amazed I haven't sat in these rocking chairs sooner." Penelope gazed out at the view, then added, "How can your work be more restful than this?"

"I like working in the garden," he replied. "To me, weeding and watering are restful activities. I just don't know if *Gott* would agree, so I try to resist on Sundays."

Penelope chuckled. "If that's the worst of your problems, you're doing pretty well."

Simon stared at his glass. Penelope didn't know about his family struggles, about his father's disapproval, about his own determination to succeed with the B&B.

She seemed to pluck his confusion out of the air, because she looked at him sharply. "Or am I wrong?" she inquired.

"Maybe," he admitted. He sighed. "I never told you how I ended up here in Montana running a B&B, did I?"

He saw wary interest on her face. "No, you haven't," she replied. "But I'd be interested in knowing."

He set his chair to rocking again and gazed out at the scenery. He took a moment or two to organize his thoughts. "I suppose you could say it all started when I was a *youngie*. A teenager," he clarified, since he doubted she was familiar with the term. "I spent a summer working at a B&B in town and enjoyed it far more than I thought I would. That's when I learned I had a knack for hospitality."

"I presume it's more than just cleaning rooms and cooking meals?"

"*Ja* sure. There's grunt work associated with any profession, of course, but I learned to 'build cathedrals' with my work."

"Build cathedrals?" She looked bewildered. "What does that mean?"

He grinned. "It's an old story about three men moving stones. A traveler asks the first man, 'What are you doing?' The man snarls, 'What does it look like I'm doing? I'm moving these stupid rocks around.' The traveler asks the second man what he is doing. The man shrugs and replies, 'What does it look like I'm doing? I'm building a wall.' The traveler asks the third man what he is doing. The man gives him a smile, lifts up his eyes and says, 'What does it look like I'm doing? I'm building a cathedral.' That's what I try to do with boring chores—build cathedrals."

She looked stunned at the story. "That's beautiful," she said softly.

He nodded and paused until her moment of reflection had passed. "Anyway, one of the things I learned while I worked at that B&B is the need to stand out in some way. The more unique you can make the business, the more it draws in customers. The unique feature could be its location—say, along a river or lake—or it could be in a popular tourist spot, or it could offer a participation package, such as customers harvesting their own vegetables or otherwise engaging in a rural experience."

"And your unique angle has to do with being off-grid?" she asked.

"*Ja*, as well as sourcing all the food locally, either from my own property or from others in church."

"That's true," she said in an odd tone. "It was certainly a factor for why I chose this one to stay in."

"After that summer, I worked for other B&Bs in the area, learning everything I could. I sparked an interest in starting one of my own one day. But my *daed*, he disagreed."

She looked puzzled. "He didn't want you running a B&B?"

"*Nein*."

"Why not?"

"Because he wanted his sons to become farmers, just as he is."

"And you didn't want to farm?"

"It's a hard life, farming. Amos can testify to that. But also, farming requires a lot of land. Property is expensive in Ohio because it's very crowded. If I started a B&B, I reasoned, I would need less land—in fact, I could just get away with having a house in town, if that's what I wanted. But *Daed*, he just brushed off those arguments and somehow seemed to think *Gott* would provide the land I needed to become a farmer."

"Is your father…?" She paused and seemed to grope for words. "Is your father a *stern* man?"

"If you mean abusive in any way, then *nein*. He's kind and cheerful and loving. But he's also opinionated, and his opinion was that farming was the best option for his sons. Amos and my other brother, Thomas, agreed, but I was the hothead. I wanted to try things my own way. It caused some conflict between my *daed* and myself," he admitted, "and I hated that. I've always gotten along with my parents, and this was the first major clash we've ever had, outside of some boyish scrapes."

"So how did you end up in Montana?"

"I followed Amos, and he followed land prices." He grinned. "Even *Daed* had to admit the truth of property prices in Ohio. We got wind of this church offering more affordable property after it purchased the ranch. Amos made some inquiries and liked what he learned, so he and Sarah uprooted and came west. I followed along, too. When I saw this house with just its three acres, I knew *Gott* had provided it for what I wanted to use it for. It's just outside the boundary of the original ranch the church had bought up, but no one else wanted it anyway because farming requires more land. Three acres is too small."

"And your father didn't want you to buy this place?"

He made a face. "*Nein.* I had saved some money, of course, but when my *grossdaddi* passed away, he left an inheritance for all his grandchildren. I wanted to use that money to start my B&B. Again, my *daed* disagreed."

"And now you have to prove yourself," she stated.

He nodded, relieved she understood. *"Ja."* He sighed. "My father is a *gut* man, but as the middle son I always feel like I'm trying to win his approval, and never felt I could live up to his expectations. It's something I've never outgrown."

"Has your father come to visit you out here?"

"*Nein.* The house isn't quite finished, as you well know. I don't want him to see it until I have my own quarters completely renovated."

"But everything else you've achieved... Simon, what you've accomplished out here is astounding. The garden itself is a tourist attraction."

"But not necessarily in the eyes of a successful farmer. The invisible work that makes a B&B worth staying in also means it's invisible to someone not in the industry. *Daed* may admit the garden looks nice, but he doesn't know what else I do to make a memorable stay for visitors. We operate in two different worlds. He may never understand or appreciate what I do."

She glanced upward at the roof of the porch, then let her gaze roam around at the yard, the lengthy driveway, the surrounding woods. "It's a hard thing to try to prove yourself," she said with feeling. "Do you think he'll ever change his mind? I mean, let's say you're booked solid for the foreseeable future and are making money hand over fist. Would that kind of success win your father's approval?"

He blinked. "I... I don't know," he stuttered. "While everyone in our church is expected to pull his own financial weight, none of us consider wealth to be a goal in itself..."

"So having your B&B become financially successful in itself wouldn't change your father's mind?"

Simon wasn't sure he liked where this line of questioning was leading. "Probably not," he admitted.

"Then what would?" she persisted. "What would create approval in your father's eyes? Becoming a farmer?"

"At this point, I don't think so," he said. "As the *Englisch* like to say, that ship has sailed."

"Then you're free," she said simply, and gave him a dazzling smile. "You're free to do whatever you want, independent of whether your father gives his approval or not. If nothing will satisfy him, then you don't have to bother trying to justify yourself in his eyes, and simply love him for the father he is, flaws and all."

She was right. Simon realized how many years he had spent in pursuit of a pipe dream, a vague hope that his career choice would redeem him in his father's eyes.

Yet Penelope had a point. If the success of his B&B wasn't hinging on trying to gain his father's approval, he could work at his own pace and only please himself—and his guests.

"You're right," he said, giving her a crooked smile. "Where did you acquire such wisdom?"

She chuckled. "I always felt—I don't know, inferior?—to my colleagues at my last job because they had college degrees and I didn't. It wasn't because of anything anyone said, it was just me. Once I realized I was the problem, not my coworkers, then my attitude improved. I was able to let go of the feeling that I had to work twice as hard just to prove my worth."

"It also makes me realize that I'll try not to be critical of whatever careers my own future children may choose," he remarked. "Everyone has to forge his own path in life, and while a father may *guide*, he can't *dictate* what his adult children do."

"That's true." She looked thoughtful. "It makes me realize how much for granted I've always taken my own parents' approval. They've always been supportive of me in whatever I do."

"That's *gut*. I've heard adoptive parents can be even more loving than natural parents, simply because they wanted a child so badly. I know Sarah's parents dote on her. It sounds like yours do, too."

Her face softened. "They're wonderful people. I've met some adopted children who are obsessed with finding their birth mother or whatever, but I never felt a lack in that regard."

"Speaking of lack…are you still feeling that sense of loss you mentioned earlier?"

She startled and went still. Her face took on an inward expression, as if she was examining something inside her. "Not as much," she finally said in a voice of wonder. "I wonder why?"

Simon suspected he knew the answer, but it wasn't his place to push. He looked at her more attentively, noting her beautiful dark eyes that seemed like windows into her soul. He was glad she had an appointment to speak to the bishop tomorrow. Whatever they would discuss between them, it might just provide her with a bit more incentive to…to…

To what? He checked the dream he was building in his mind. To convert and become Amish? To stay and let him court her? "Idiot," he muttered to himself.

He acknowledged that Penelope was more than just a guest at his B&B. The unbelievable coincidence of finding her long-lost twin sister was proof that *Gott* had His hand in her being here. But to build hopes that Penelope was the one for him…well, that was stretching credulity too far.

Chapter Eleven

Penelope looked forward to talking with the bishop. Having obtained easy directions from Simon as to how to find the church leader's home, she set off walking on Monday afternoon.

She looked around as she walked. This section of Montana was so very different than the urban life she'd led in Boston, or even the quiet suburban neighborhood in which she'd grown up in Pennsylvania. Here the road was gravel, there were no billboards or even overhead power lines, and the scattered homes and farms were set well off the road. Between the bands of conifers, cows grazed in broad fields.

It took her about half an hour to get to the Beilers' home, which looked like a made-over barn with a wide lawn in front. A large vegetable garden, fenced tall against deer, was next to the lawn. Penelope walked up the porch steps and knocked on the door.

A short plump woman, her gray hair tucked neatly under her *kapp*, answered. "*Guten tag*, Penelope."

"Lois Beiler, right?" Penelope vaguely remembered meeting the bishop's wife, but there were so many new faces in the church that they tended to blur.

"*Ja*, you are right. *Komm* in. My *hutband* is in the

kitchen, lingering over some apple pie I made for lunch. Would you care for a piece?"

"No, thank you. Simon makes such excellent breakfasts that it usually carries me right through until dinner."

Lois chuckled and led the way through the home toward the kitchen.

As indicated, the older man was seated at the table, an empty dessert plate and cup of coffee before him. He rose as she entered the kitchen. "*Guten tag*, Penelope. Would you like some coffee?"

She hesitated. "*Tea* would be lovely."

"Tea it is," Lois said, and began preparing the beverage.

"You have a beautiful home," offered Penelope, glancing around at the kitchen.

"*Ja*, it's a nice place for just the two of us. My niece and her *hutband* live in the place just next door, so we have some young *kinner* we can spoil." He smiled and sipped his coffee.

"I feel the same way about Sarah's children. All this time, I had no idea I had a niece and nephew. I think because of our physical similarities, the kids have become very comfortable with me."

"That is quite a story, having you and Sarah randomly meet. I see the hand of *Gott* in it."

"I… I do, too." Penelope swallowed. "And that's difficult for me to admit. I wasn't raised in faith of any sort. My parents weren't against it, you understand, but neither really went to church except maybe on the high holidays. I've never really given faith much thought one way or the other…until now."

"Since you are involved in what could almost be seen

as a literal miracle, I can understand that," remarked the bishop.

"Simon is the first one who pointed it out," Penelope replied thoughtfully. "He said, what are the odds of me choosing his particular B&B for a stay? The more I thought about it, the more I think he might be right. Thank you," she added to Lois as the older woman placed a mug on the table. "Or maybe I should say, *danke.*"

The bishop chuckled. "Sarah mentioned you speak a little German?"

"Yes, I studied the language in high school and a little beyond. I got really into it for a while and even took a trip to Germany a few years ago, where I managed to get by, but it's been a long time and most of it has left me." Penelope smiled. "It makes following the church service a little challenging. Which brings me to one of the reasons I'm here," she added. "I wanted to talk over a few issues with you."

"Is this a private matter? We can go into my office."

"No, it's not private at all. I'm just curious, and it leads to what you talked about yesterday in church. I may have misunderstood you since my German is so poor, but did you use the term *called*?"

"Gerufen? Ja."

"And does that mean what I think it means? Does God 'call' people? How could that even happen?"

"It happens all the time," the church leader replied.

Penelope couldn't quite accept his simple belief. "I looked it up in the index of the Bible Simon left in my room and found something that says being called by name. What does that mean?"

"'Fear not: for I have redeemed thee, I have called

thee by thy name; thou art mine,'" quoted the bishop with a smile. "A powerful passage indeed."

"But what does it *mean*?" she asked with a trace of impatience. "Why do I keep thinking about it?"

"Originally it was directed at an entire nation," replied the bishop. "But the power of those words can also be interpreted at an individual level. *Gott* can call people to believe in Him. Now let me ask you something. Why did that particular term stay in your mind to the point where you wanted to ask me about it?"

Penelope answered slowly, "Because I can't help but feel that passage is being directed at me."

He nodded. "The very fact that you're asking means you might be feeling that call."

"How would I know?"

"It takes some reflection," the older man advised. "You must look inside yourself. Have you felt an emptiness or felt like something was missing? Sometimes what's missing is faith in *Gott*. Then you— What's wrong?" he added in alarm.

Penelope felt the blood drain from her face. "How did you know?" she whispered. How could the bishop have known about that lifelong sense of loss?

"Know what?" The man looked bewildered.

Penelope gave a small shake of her head, trying to dispel the chill that went down her spine. "I've felt that," she admitted. "For as long as I can remember, I felt something was missing. When I met Sarah, I wondered if that sensation sprang from an unconscious longing for my twin, but as much as I've come to love my sister, that feeling didn't go away. The only time I've felt it lessen is in church, even though I don't understand much of what's being said."

"I see." The bishop folded his hands on the table. "This is turning into something interesting. Has it occurred to you that your sense of loss stems from a lack of faith?"

"Simon suggested as much." Penelope heard the slight tremble in her voice, and strove to control it. "But I'm assuming faith isn't something that can be turned on or off like a switch. How does someone acquire faith?"

"Mostly through practice," said the older man. "You're already taking the first steps by coming to church, though I understand the language barrier makes it difficult. The next step would be to read. Read an *Englisch* Bible so you can understand it more completely. And you might read other books, too, about how other people found their faith. Or books that are instructive in faith."

"Simon had a good-sized selection of books in the library, a very eclectic mixture. Fiction, nonfiction, and I'm sure I've seen some books about religion in there. I'll look more closely."

"As I see it—" the bishop sipped his coffee "—you have an identical twin sister who is Amish. From what I understand, your birth mother was Amish. You've been slipping very easily into an Amish community. Have you thought about staying longer?"

"Yes," she said in a heartfelt voice. "But…but I have obligations that may pull me away. I have to admit, it's sending me into some confusion. Bishop, here's a strange question, but…how many people convert and become Amish?"

"Not many," he admitted. "And it's not a strange question at all. I get asked it all the time, but mostly by people who are interested in the superficial aspects of our culture. Most find they can't handle the lack of modern conveniences and the physical labor. Some are dismayed to discover we're not perfect, but instead are simply human, with all the flaws and problems that humans have. Not many would-be converts are interested in the deeper dive about how we live by our faith."

"So this calling I might feel probably has nothing to do with being called to become Amish."

"I doubt it." A brief smile came and went on the older man's face. "But everything would have to start with faith anyway. If you want my advice, Miss Moore, it's this: if you're being called, *listen*."

Simon sat on a crate before a raised bed of carrots, weeding. The bed hardly needed it but he persisted for two reasons. One, the garden was part of the appeal of his business. Almost every visitor wanted a tour. It behooved him to keep the garden as handsome and tidy as possible.

And two, weeding was his prayer time. It was what he did when he faced an issue or needed some guidance.

He had already checked in a new guest, a cheerful and rotund middle-aged man named Leonard Baskin who somehow managed to convey a sense of personal power, as if he was in charge of important things. He was here to visit relatives, he told Simon, and to attend a nephew's wedding in town. He planned to stay a week.

"Are you Amish?" he asked in some surprise as he checked in.

"Ja," replied Simon. "We're a fairly new settlement. Most of us come from Ohio and Indiana."

"My company is based in Indianapolis," the man said, "so I've seen quite a number of Amish in my day."

Simon settled Mr. Baskin into his room, explained the meal schedule, told him about some of the local amenities he might like to explore and then came downstairs to put on some beans to soak for tomorrow's soup. Then he went outside to weed.

But his thoughts were focused on one thing, or rather one person: Penelope. What was she talking over with the bishop? He would never ask, of course. It wasn't any of his business. But he prayed the bishop might be guiding her toward…well, toward what he, Simon, wanted. Then he prayed for forgiveness for the selfishness of that prayer.

He wanted Penelope to stay. At the same time, he knew the folly of that wish. Why oh why did he have to set his heart on an *Englisch* woman? As much as his guest resembled his sister-in-law—and as much as Penelope looked Amish while attired in Sarah's borrowed clothing—Simon couldn't focus on those superficial veneers.

Courting her was out of the question. Not only was he a baptized member of the church—he had taken his vows years ago—but he had no interest in leaving. He loved his church, he was a man of faith and he knew the cold consequences should he violate the rules of the *Ordnung*.

But could Penelope actually convert? That was a lot to ask—not only in embracing a faith that was foreign to her, but in embracing a lifestyle that was even more so.

So he weeded, tidying the already neat garden beds, while his mind churned in confusion and he begged *Gott* for a solution. Frankly he could see none that wouldn't result in heartache of one kind or another.

A crunch of gravel interrupted his thoughts. His heart gave a leap as he watched Penelope approach, a thoughtful expression on her face.

He straightened up, still sitting on the crate. "Welcome back. Just so you know, we have another guest staying, a very nice middle-aged man. How went your meeting with the bishop?"

"It was...interesting. May I join you?" she added, gesturing toward another crate.

"*Ja* sure." He didn't try to dissuade his guest from dirtying her hands in the soil. For all he knew, Penelope found as much comfort in the mindless task as he did.

"You look—I don't know—confused?" he offered. He desperately wanted to know the content of her conversation with the church leader, but wasn't about to ask.

"Yes, I guess I am. He's an interesting man, your bishop. I like him. He's not preachy, but you can tell he's very learned about his position. I was impressed."

"He's a *gut* man," agreed Simon. "He has a challenging job, guiding this mishmash of new settlers from many different churches from many different states. He also has a natural counseling skill that can be very helpful, as you can imagine."

"So I noticed. Simon..." She kept her head bent over the plants. "Have you ever felt called?"

"Called?" he repeated. "As in, called to do something?"

"Maybe, but what I mean is, called by God?"

He felt something leap inside him, but he kept his face impassive and his voice calm. "*Ja*, of course. I was called to be baptized when I was a younger man. I was called to become an innkeeper."

"Well, that's one of the things the bishop and I discussed—what it means to be called. That's what he talked about yesterday in his sermon, and since it was kind of hard for me to follow everything he said in German, I wanted to make sure I didn't mishear or misunderstand his meaning."

"Is that what you're feeling now?" he asked cautiously. It seemed too close to an answer to his own prayer and he didn't want to develop any false hope.

"I don't know," she replied with a trace of annoyance in her voice, something he instinctively understood wasn't directed at him but instead at her own emotions. "Bishop Beiler said that if I feel called, I need to *listen*. But I don't know how. It leaves me confused and even a bit irritated."

"Did he have any advice on what to do?"

"He suggested attending church, of course, but since the language barrier is still an issue, he also wanted me to do some reading—the Bible and any other books that might be helpful." She jerked her head toward the house. "I saw an interesting selection of books on your bookshelf in the lobby. Do you have anything you can recommend?"

"*Ja*, I do. There's also an *Englisch* phrase you're no doubt familiar with—'Fake it till you make it.' In other words, a real belief might follow on the heels of *acting* like you're following the faith. Does that make sense?"

"Yes, I guess so." She shrugged. "And it's not like I have any better ideas. All I know is this…this *tug* won't leave me alone. I suppose I'd better pay attention to my gut."

"Or pay attention to what *Gott* is saying," he ventured. "But, Penelope…this all takes time. How much longer can you stay? Not that I'm trying to hurry you out," he added hastily, "because I'm not. But I was under the impression you weren't going to be here much longer."

She scowled more fiercely. "I'm still working that out. I don't feel ready to leave. I mean, I just discovered I have a long-lost twin sister. How could I leave her so soon after meeting her? But I have…commitments that may not permit me to stay."

Privately Simon wondered what kind of commitments a freelance artist—who seemed as footloose and fancy-free as he could imagine—could have that would tear her away from a newfound sister, but it wasn't his place to ask. She had mentioned having debt, and since her arrival here he had seen no indication she was selling any of the paintings she was creating. For all he knew, she had some financial pressure that compelled her to leave.

He sighed. It underscored the folly of developing any romantic interest in her—there was so much about her he didn't know. There seemed to be some distant and vague secret force that was driving her away. He wished he knew what it was.

"Well." He stood up and dusted off his hands. "I should get dinner started."

"What are you making? Maybe I can help."

"Broccoli salad and potato pancakes." He cocked his head at her. "It requires a lot of chopping and shredding. Another pair of hands is always welcome."

"Sure!" She smiled and dusted off her own hands. "I miss cooking. I used to do it quite a bit."

"Let's start by harvesting what we need." Simon

fetched two baskets and a knife. "If you want to cut the broccoli heads, I'm going to dig up some new potatoes."

It was a pleasant experience harvesting fresh vegetables with her. Per his directions, she clipped a fair number of broccoli heads, pulled several red onions and harvested a cabbage. Meanwhile he dug a fair number of potatoes from the mounded earth, yanked a couple of yellow onions and snipped some fresh parsley.

"This is the way it's supposed to be done," she remarked as she followed him into the kitchen. "Local organic food. And you're an amazing chef, Simon."

"Well, technically I'm an amazing *cook*," he replied with a smile. "A chef is specially trained. The only training I got was from my *graemmaemm*."

He showed her how to dip the broccoli in salt water to remove any insects, then joined her in peeling, dicing and shredding.

"'Many hands make light work,'" he quoted at one point. "I must admit, it's a lot more fun having company in the kitchen."

"Yes," she agreed. "I'd forgotten how much I enjoy working with others. That barn raising was…amazing. I can't even begin to tell you how much I enjoyed working with the other women."

"Then you've caught a glimpse of what I said earlier," he replied, "about subsuming one's identity to that of the community as an expression of our faith."

"I see." She looked thoughtful.

Simon hardly dared hope that she did, indeed, "see." *Call her more loudly, Gott*, he prayed.

Chapter Twelve

The next morning, Penelope sat in the dining room at a separate table from Leonard Baskin, the portly middle-aged man she had met the evening before at dinner. He politely greeted her, then buried himself in a newspaper.

Abruptly she heard a knock on the front door. Simon, working in the kitchen, snapped his head up, dusted off his hands and hurried to answer it.

From her vantage point in the dining room, she could just see Simon as he opened the door.

"Hello," a man's voice said. "My name is Ed Holmes. Sorry to drop in without reservations, but we were passing through town to look at some real estate and we'll be in the area for a couple of days. An Amish lady at a store in town recommended your B&B. Do you have room for a family with two kids?"

Simon's face took on what Penelope was starting to call his "hospitality expression": a blend of friendliness and professionalism. "*Ja*, of course," he said, standing back to welcome the visitors inside. "I have a connected suite with two bedrooms and a shared bathroom. Will that suit?"

"Perfectly!" said a well-coiffed woman whom Penelope could just glimpse around the corner of the room. She glanced around. "So much nicer than the motel on the other side of town."

"I'm just serving breakfast to my guests," offered Simon. "Have you eaten? Or I can show you to your rooms right away?"

"We haven't eaten," said the man. "What do you say, dear? Would you like to have breakfast here?"

"Yes, please," the woman replied. "It smells delicious."

"Then let me seat you, and afterward I'll check you in and assist you with your luggage," said Simon.

He walked into the dining room with the family on his heels. The children, both girls, looked to be around six and eight years old.

Simon made introductions. "I'm Simon Troyer," he said. "These are my guests Penelope Moore and Leonard Baskin. Ed Holmes, you said?"

"Yes," said the man, "and this is my wife, Emily, and our daughters, Nancy and Noelle."

"How do you do?" said Penelope politely. The family seemed pleasant.

After the greetings, Simon seated the family at a large table, poured out beverages, and brought out an abundant amount of bacon, eggs, toast and hash browns.

Sipping the last of her tea, she watched Simon at work. It was impossible to fault him for anything—his manners, his welcome, his service, his cooking. The family seemed appreciative. He knew when to linger for a moment's conversation and when to retreat to let the family eat in peace.

She tried to view his activities through the eyes of a dispassionate observer, and honestly she couldn't see anything he did that required improvement. What benefit could he gain from coming under the QuirkyB&B umbrella? She could see nothing.

"There goes your commission," she muttered to herself, annoyed but resigned. The longer she stayed at Simon's establishment, the less of a dream job QuirkyB&B—with its emphasis on high-pressure tactics—seemed to be. The last thing she wanted to do was bully Simon into making a financial decision to benefit *her*, but clearly would not especially help *him*.

Yet that crushingly large credit card bill still lingered. She had made a minimum payment on it, which she knew would barely touch the principal of what she owed.

It was a depressing thought, but not a new one. Penelope simply didn't know what to do about it. When she was frustrated or troubled, she had an urge to paint to calm herself down. A special piece that was nearly finished sat on her easel up in her room. It seemed as good a time to complete it as any.

She carried her dishes to the service window. "I'm going to do some painting," she told Simon, who was scrubbing a pan. She added in German, "Let me know if you need any help with the new guests."

"Ja, danke," he replied with a twinkle in his eye.

Nodding to the chattering family and the middle-aged man, she made her way upstairs and closed her bedroom door behind her. Donning her smock, she put brush to canvas.

The piece was almost finished. It was the fifth painting she had done since arriving, and so far one of her favorites...in part because it featured Simon working in the garden.

He had no idea how often she watched him from her window as he weeded or watered or harvested. She had sketched him several times until one rough sketch gelled and she knew it would be the focus of her painting. In it, he stood with his characteristic straw hat and suspenders, picking pea pods with efficiency, a full basket on the ground next to him, while a bounty of other vegetables were visible in the background—climbing beans and corn and tomatoes and squash. Those beautifully fresh peas had appeared in that evening's dinner, as had other vegetables he had harvested, and she felt intimidated by the extent of his skills in running this establishment.

When the painting was finished, she intended to gift it to Simon…just as she intended to gift Sarah with another painting showing her hanging wash on a clothesline with her children playing at her feet.

The simple domestic scenes of the various sketches she had turned into paintings pleased her. It seemed to wash her soul after the urban chaos that was her life in Boston. More and more, she wished nothing more than the chance to stay here, to get to know her sister better, to delve into the community's spiritual side…and to stay close to Simon.

She sighed and paused on a brushstroke. Staying close to Simon was on her mind a lot lately.

In short, everything was tugging at her to stay…with one exception. She glared at the credit card bill on her bedside table.

Voices came from the stairwell. Simon was showing the new family to their room. The suite, she knew by now, lay at the opposite end of the house. Penelope smiled as a child's voice piped, "Chickens, Mommy! He has chickens in the back! Can we see them?"

"You'll have to ask him later, Nancy," the mother replied in a reproving tone. "He has work to do and we don't want to disturb him."

"Once you settle in," said Simon, "I'd be happy to give you a garden tour. The children can even collect some eggs if they want."

Penelope smiled at the resulting squeals of excitement from the kids.

"Thank you," Emily Holmes replied. The voices faded into indistinct chatter as the family moved down the hall toward their room.

Suddenly her phone rang. Penelope suppressed a flutter of dread at the thought it might be her supervisor at QuirkyB&B. However a quick glance at the screen showed it was her parents' phone number.

Penelope put them on speakerphone so she could continue painting. "Hi, Mom!"

"And Dad," her father called, and she chuckled. Her parents were also on speakerphone.

"How's life in Montana?" inquired Angie.

"It's great," replied Penelope, dabbing at the canvas. "Believe it or not, I'm getting a fair bit of painting done. I'll have to send you photos of some of the pieces I've finished. The guy who runs the B&B is a sweetheart and my sister is everything I could hope for. I hope you guys have a chance to meet her sometime."

"We do, too," replied Walter. "And in fact, it's your sister we're calling about, at least indirectly. Honey, we've made all kinds of inquiries about the adoption agency, and simply can't find much. The people running it seem to have disappeared. We don't have the money to hire a lawyer or detective to track anyone down."

"Don't go into debt for this!" exclaimed Penelope in alarm. She plunked her brush into a jar of water. "No matter what you find out, good or bad, it won't bring back the missed years. Don't let it trouble you. I just wish…" She trailed off.

"Wish what, honey?" Her mother's voice was gentle.

Penelope decided to be honest. "I wish I could ditch this new job and just paint for a living, and stay here. Oh, Mom, Dad, this new community is really something. We had a lot of Amish people around us growing up, but we never really had much to do with them. But in part because of Sarah, they've welcomed me as no community has ever welcomed me before. I just feel this urge to stay…and of course, to stay near Sarah."

"So the only thing preventing you from quitting is that credit card bill hanging over your head?" asked her father in a thoughtful voice.

"Pretty much. I thought it would be a shoo-in to live cheaply since the job was covering my basic living expenses, and the commissions would have given me a financial cushion. But now that I'm on my first job, I'm not sure I like it. No wonder they were always hiring," she added with some sarcasm.

Her father gave a rusty chuckle. "Yes, businesses which are always hiring usually have a high turnover rate for a reason. But is there a job you can get locally? Something that would allow you to stay in Montana?"

"I've thought about it. Sarah even offered to let me stay with them so I wouldn't have to pay rent." She sighed. "There's a lot of uncertainty and a lot of stuff to think over. It would be a lot simpler if I didn't have this credit card bill hanging over my head. You guys were right to preach against the evils of debt. It really limits choices in life."

"We all make mistakes, honey," said her father gently. "Don't beat yourself up over it."

"Now tell me what's going on at your end," said Penelope.

For half an hour, she chatted with her parents about what was happening. Then she said goodbye, hung up and stared aimlessly at the nearly finished canvas.

Her thoughts ricocheted all over the place. Gratitude and love for the people who raised her as their own child. A more insightful understanding of the evils and dangers of being in debt. And above all, a desperate wish that she could stay here, doing what she was doing, without the looming threat of missing out on the commission she was counting on to pay off her bills.

She bit her lip. She couldn't see a solution to her problem.

When Simon passed by Penelope's closed door, he could hear her on the phone with a man and a woman he quickly determined were her parents. What caused him to become rooted to the spot and eavesdrop, he didn't know…but he quickly realized there was more to Penelope than met the eye. Or in this case, the ears.

She wanted to "ditch this new job" but she couldn't quit because of the credit card bill hanging over her head. This mysterious job was covering her basic living expenses, which meant the cost of her long-term stay at his B&B was being paid for by someone else. And she was on commission.

What did it mean? He knew she was an artist—he'd seen her work and recognized her talent—but now it seemed her art was simply a cover for something else, something on commission, something that required her to stay for a long time at a remote B&B in a wild corner of Montana.

He descended the stairs in a thoughtful frame of mind that gradually changed into irritation. He realized how little he actually knew her, and mentally chastised himself for developing an interest in the *Englischer*. No matter how much she might resemble her devout sister, Penelope didn't have the foundation of faith, like a rock beneath her feet, that might keep her from behaving unethically.

He scowled at the empty kitchen. Speaking of foundation, it seemed he had been building a castle in the air by entertaining hopes and dreams about Penelope. He had no foundation, no rock base, no common ground with this woman beyond her superficial resemblance to his sister-in-law.

He was a fool to build any long-term plans around her.

But even as he mentally retreated from their budding friendship, his mind rebelled, and it took him a few minutes to realize why.

He was lonely.

Surrounded as he was by a vibrant and supportive community of church members, he had no one of his own. He wanted a wife. He wanted children. And he had foolishly begun to believe Penelope could fill that gap within him.

He snorted at his own folly. No wonder the *Ordnung* was strict about marrying within one's own faith. It was dangerous to stray off the path.

Unless and until he knew more about Penelope's reason for being here, he would treat her with professional courtesy, and no more.

He heard the chatter as the Holmes family descended the stairs, and put aside his personal issues to become the hospitable host that was expected from him.

"If the offer to tour the garden is still available, I'd love to take you up on it," said Emily Holmes.

Her two daughters tugged at her shirt. "Chickens, Mama, chickens!" said the youngest one earnestly in a stage whisper.

"And the girls have done nothing but talk about the chickens," added Emily with a smile.

"The chickens are very friendly," replied Simon. "The only thing we have to be careful about is not to let them out of their pen so they don't get in among the vegetables."

He led the way out back and watched as the children exclaimed over the poultry. For the briefest moment they were *his* kids. Then he shook his head to dispel the vision. He didn't have *kinner*, and at this stage he wondered if he ever would. At the moment, his niece and nephew were the closest he would get.

He toured the family around the garden and inquired about their interest in quiche for dinner. Emily Holmes delighted in cutting the broccoli and pulling the onions he would use, and the children collected the eggs necessary for the dish. Simon promised them dinner at six o'clock, and the family finally piled into their car and departed for their real estate appointments, leaving a peaceful quiet in their wake as he started preparing dinner.

No sooner had the Holmes departed when Leonard Baskin also descended the stairs. "I'm off to visit my friends," he told Simon. "What time do you normally serve dinner?"

"Six o'clock," Simon replied. "Quiche all right with you?"

"Yes, that sounds wonderful." The man plopped a hat on his nearly bald head and left the building. Simon heard his car start up and depart.

"Are they gone?" inquired a voice.

He looked up to see Penelope smiling at him through the service window of the kitchen.

His heart skipped a beat at seeing her until he remembered his promise to stay distant.

"Ja," he replied. "Nice family. I gather they have several real estate appointments over the next few days. Everyone will be here for dinner. How goes the painting?" he couldn't help but ask. He washed broccoli and began chopping it up.

"It's going well." He glanced up in time to see a troubled look on her face. "I have a painting I hope to give to Sarah. It shows her hanging clothes with the kids playing at her feet. No one's face shows," she added hastily.

"Ja gut. The *Ordnung* is pretty clear about photography."

"Why is that, anyway?" she asked curiously.

"It's too close to making graven images," he replied.

"I see." She looked thoughtful, then added, "Need any help?"

"With dinner? *Nein.* I have to remember you're a guest, not an employee."

He wanted to kick himself at the stricken look on her face. "Arguably I'm family," she said in a hurt tone. "But okay. Since you don't want help, I guess I'll return to painting."

And whatever mysterious job you have, he thought, and wondered anew what it could be. He had seen no evidence of any other work—no computer, no paperwork—and as far as he could tell she simply focused on her art as well as her newfound family and community connections.

It was a mystery. He wasn't sure he liked mysteries.

But he didn't want to be cold or professional with her. He liked her personally, and it pained him to hurt her in any way.

So he chopped and diced and created a dinner from the products of his garden and chickens, and wished he had company in the kitchen. Last night's assistance was more than just meal preparation. Shared tasks were always more enjoyable.

But he was now determined to hold her at arm's length. There was too much uncertainty about her—now more than ever.

He paused a moment and leaned over the cutting board. *Why,* Gott, *why?* he thought. Why send him a woman who was the first person he'd had a serious interest in courting, only for it to be impossible to court her? Unmarried women of his faith were scarce here in the Montana settlement. Would he have to go back to Ohio to find a wife?

He couldn't leave his business long enough to find and court someone. Perhaps his parents could recommend a woman. There was almost too much of an age gap now with the unmarried women in his old town, but perhaps there was a young widow who might be interested in settling in Montana.

The thought left him cold. He couldn't garner a single ounce of interest in the thought of a long-distance courtship.

For a brief moment he entertained the thought of leaving the church in order to court Penelope. Immediately his mind recoiled at the thought. He would be shunned without mercy. He would leave behind his brother and sister-in-law, his niece and nephew, his parents and all the dear people he'd grown up with. He would be giving up so much. Was Penelope worth it?

Nein. Simon thinned his lips and began chopping vegetables with a vengeance. And if his eyes were watering, he blamed it on the onions.

Chapter Thirteen

❧

"This is for me?" Simon's jaw dropped.

"Yes."

It was Wednesday morning after a late breakfast. The rest of the guests had departed for a few hours, and the house was quiet. Then, after the dishes were washed, Penelope said, "Wait here. I've got something for you."

She had finished the canvas last night. It was never her intention to keep it for herself. She knew from the first time she sketched it out that it was for Simon.

She couldn't explain why she so badly wanted to gift him with her talent, but she did. She had read something the other day about listening when she heard a "still, small voice." Well, that still, small voice within her prompted her to dedicate a painting to Simon, so she did.

Now, as she watched his face when he realized he was the subject of the artwork, she felt a flush of happiness.

"I hope you don't mind," she said. "The view from my window is so beautiful, and one day I saw you out there picking peas. I made a quick sketch, and then transferred it to a canvas."

His throat worked and she thought she saw a suspicious sheen of moisture in his eyes. "I don't know what to say, Penelope. You have so much talent."

"It's what God gave me." She shrugged.

He shot a look at her. "What *Gott* gave you?" he repeated.

"Yes." She felt shy admitting it. "I was painting this and wondering where I got my talent. My parents aren't interested in art, so I wonder if my birth mother was? But then Sarah says she has no artistic talent, either, although I think her quilts are beautiful. So where else could I have gotten the urge or skill to paint except as a gift from God?"

He chuckled. "I like your logic. Truly this is beautiful. I'd like to hang it in the lobby, if that's all right with you."

"Of course. I'll admit, there's enough scenery around here to keep me painting for a lifetime." She wished there was an actual way to do just that, but she couldn't see how.

"There." Simon pointed to a spot on the wall above the large lobby bookcase. "It would look perfect in that location."

Within a few minutes he had located the necessary tools and had the painting hung on the wall. Penelope directed him from across the room to level it properly.

Finally Simon came to stand next to her and view the painting from the span of the room. There was a moment's silence.

"Beautiful," he repeated at last. "I'm humbled you chose me as a subject for a painting."

"I knew better than to show your face," she said. "Same with the painting I plan to give to Sarah, where she's hanging clothes on the line with the children at her feet."

"It's no wonder you can afford to be a traveling artist," Simon remarked with a certain strange emphasis to the words. "The quality of your work is amazing."

It was all Penelope could do to keep from shrinking into the woodwork behind her. *If only*, she thought. *If only he knew, if only it were true, if only...* She bit her lip in vexation.

"What's wrong?"

She looked over to see Simon watching her. "Nothing," she lied. "Just...wondering."

"Wondering what?"

Penelope decided on a modicum of truth. "Wondering what it would take to stay here longer than I planned. I feel so at home here, among this community and the people I've met so far. And of course, I like being close to Sarah. I hate the thought of leaving her behind."

"I know she would love to have you stay longer. And so would..." His voice trailed off.

She glanced at him sharply. "And so would what?" Maybe it was her imagination, but it seemed the air was suddenly charged with something beyond polite professionalism. It seemed the chemistry she imagined wasn't just on her side.

"And so would I," he said in a low voice.

Apparently her interest in Simon wasn't as one-sided as she'd thought. Why hadn't he said anything? In the urban world she had left behind, attraction between two people was acted on with sometimes incautious speed. But Simon had kept his thoughts to himself, never hinting his role as a hotelier had changed into something else.

But now, through several heartbeats of silence, she looked into his dark blue eyes and saw a degree of silent suffering that startled her. Had he planned to never say anything? Could she just have moved on to another assignment, blithely unaware that he harbored feelings for her?

She swallowed. "This changes everything, doesn't it?"

"I don't know." He clenched his fists. "You're off-limits on so many levels that it leaves me frustrated."

"Off-limits?"

"*Ja*. You're not Amish. I could no more court you than I could court a movie star without the risk of being shunned."

Shunned. So that was it. She'd heard the term, but for the first time she considered the full implications of it. If Simon was shunned, he would be excluded from everything he held dear—his family, his friends, his community, his church, his faith. It was a lot to risk over the clear chemistry between them.

Unconsciously she took a step back, putting more space between them. "I would never ask that of you," she said quietly. "I couldn't bear the thought of being forcibly separated from my parents, or even my new-found sister. It would be a hundred times worse for you."

He looked at the floor. "*Ja,*" he replied. "It would be. And believe me when I say that's what prevents me from doing or saying anything inappropriate. But from the first time I… No, never mind." He abruptly spun on his heel. "I have work to do."

He practically ran from the room into his private quarters. The door closed firmly behind him.

From the first time he what? The first time they met? The first time he introduced her to Sarah? The first time he *what*?

Had she crossed a line by giving him a painting? It was certainly a personal thing, very much a gift from the heart.

From the heart…

Abruptly Penelope dropped down in one of the lobby chairs and stared at the painting. Was that what this was? Was she falling for Simon?

This possibility added a whole new level of complexity to what was already a complex situation. The difference in faith was the least of her worries. What worried her more was what Simon would think when she revealed why she was truly here. It would be a betrayal of epic proportions, since essentially her purpose here was an effort to snatch his burgeoning business out from under him.

But putting aside the worries over her job, she had to admit the truth: yes, she was falling for Simon.

It was hard not to. The man had so many stellar qualities. His quiet confidence somehow made him seem stronger and more admirable than all the brash coworkers she worked with at the marketing agency. Those men had a tendency to live a flashier lifestyle, hinting if not outright bragging about their salaries, and firmly committed to climbing the corporate ladder.

But while Simon was clearly motivated to make his business successful—and possibly prove something to his father—he didn't do so from a position of ego. And that, she realized, was an unbelievably attractive quality.

But he was off-limits. He'd said as much. The chasm between them was too wide to breach. It was bad enough that she was here to talk him into franchising his business. It would be a thousand times worse if she did something that would cause him to be shunned by his church.

For a moment, she glimpsed the enormity of how her actions could impact the larger community if she was to entice Simon into inappropriate behavior. Her sister would be horrified. She, Penelope, would be given the cold shoulder from everyone, starting with the bishop.

It was truly a "village" situation, in which expected standards of behavior kept members from straying too far off the path. Such a situation had its drawbacks, yes, but it also had its advantages. She admired Simon for his forbearance in considering her off-limits. It meant that he didn't indulge in flings or other regrettable behavior.

For that reason, she would never encourage him to behave in a way contrary to his faith or his beliefs.

Faith and beliefs…

Maybe it was time to learn more about Amish faith and beliefs, to learn more about what her birth mother came from and what her twin sister was raised in. But how?

Her eyes moved from the painting to the bookshelf beneath. She had scanned the titles at various times during her stay and borrowed a few volumes to read in her room. But now she looked through them with more focus. Sure enough, there were two or three volumes on Amish culture. She flipped open one and scanned the table of contents, then snapped it closed and carried it upstairs to her bedroom.

Maybe it was time to learn a little more about this community in which she found herself ensconced— either by accident or, as Simon put it, by the hand of God.

Simon shut the door to his private quarters behind him, then leaned against it, closed his eyes and pinched the bridge of his nose.

He hadn't meant to confess his feelings to her. Doing

so altered their entire relationship. No longer could she view him as a professional hotelier, or even a brother-in-law of sorts. Instead, he was a man who admired and esteemed her—and would even court her if that one insurmountable barrier wasn't between them.

And it *was* a barrier. Simon had been baptized years ago. Until this moment, he had never even considered doing anything that would violate the terms of those vows.

What was it about Penelope that attracted him? He'd never felt anything but brotherly feelings for his sister-in-law Sarah. But her identical twin captured his fancy in a way he'd never expected. He tried not to become obsessed with her or view her in any other light except that of a guest and a relative of sorts.

And then, of course, there was this mystery job of hers...

He was glad he had a meeting with the bishop this afternoon. The church leader would know what to say to knock some sense into him.

Simon made sure to stay out of Penelope's sight until he deemed it was the right time to start walking toward the Beilers' farm. He plopped his straw hat on his head, tugged his suspenders straight and set out on the road.

Summer was advancing and the grasses were turning yellow. A couple of times he even caught a glimpse of early autumn, usually by the smell of the breeze. Sometimes he missed the eternal green summers of Ohio, where it rained constantly, but he didn't miss the humidity. The west was much drier, but it had its charm.

The Amish district was looking more settled. Meadows had been fenced for cattle or horses, barns and homes were more established, and he frequently saw children and *youngies* at leisure. He loved the snug feeling of community the settlement offered.

He frowned. That affection for the church community was the reason he was going to see the bishop. He didn't want to jeopardize his position in it over an *Englischer*.

Soon enough he arrived at the bishop's residence. Samuel and his wife, Lois, were sitting in rockers on the front porch, a frosty pitcher on a table between them. He felt a pang as he watched them chat quietly. Would he ever sit on a porch rocker in his senior years beside a helpmeet to whom he had been married for decades? At the moment, it didn't seem possible.

"*Guder nammidaag*, Samuel. Lois," greeted Simon as he drew near.

"*Guder nammidaag,*" they replied in unison. Samuel added, "A glass of iced tea for you?"

"*Ja, bitte.*"

Lois stood up to fetch another glass. In her brief absence, the church leader asked, "Is the subject you want to discuss private, or can Lois sit in?"

Simon considered a moment. Having a woman's perspective might not be a bad idea. "As long as you understand the matter is confidential, I don't mind Lois hearing me out."

"You have my word. Ah, *danke*, *lieb*," the bishop added as Lois emerged from the house with an ice-filled glass. She poured tea and handed the tumbler to Simon.

"I was just telling Samuel that I wouldn't mind your perspective if I can assume you'll both keep the matter confidential," Simon said to Lois as he pulled another rocker over.

"*Ja*, of course." Lois smiled at him. Simon knew her to be just as discreet as her husband.

"It's about Penelope," he stated bluntly. "I'm sure it doesn't come as a surprise to either of you that I've developed feelings for her."

He saw the bishop's nostrils flare as if in surprise, but the older man said nothing.

Into the silence, Lois Beiler ventured, "And how strong are these feelings, Simon?"

"Strong enough to leave me confused and angry with myself," he confessed. "This morning, Penelope presented me with a painting she had done of me working in the garden. It's a beautiful canvas, and I hung it in the lobby. Somehow the subject shifted from admiration of the painting to admiration of her, and now she knows. *Schtupid*," he added to himself in a furious voice.

"This is problematic," admitted the bishop. He took a sip of tea. "And I don't need to tell you the reasons why."

"*Nein*, you don't. Believe me, I'm familiar with every single barrier in existence. I… I guess I don't know what there is to discuss with you," he finished awkwardly. "There isn't anything you can say I don't already know."

"Except one thing." The church leader regarded him with some sympathy. "As you know, I had an earlier meeting with Penelope, in which she wanted an explanation for what I touched on in the Sunday sermon, namely the issue of being called. I find it interesting."

"Called toward becoming Amish?"

"*Nein*, called toward faith. Just faith in general. Without giving away too much in confidence, she seems to have a longing to become more acquainted with the subject."

"I know she's been doing some reading on the topic." He sighed. "I just wish I knew where it would lead."

"At the moment, it will lead to nothing *gut*," warned the bishop. "She's not Amish."

"Simon…" Lois Beiler leaned forward, a concerned look on her face. "You've only known Penelope a short time."

"Ja und nein," he replied. "I've known Sarah practically my whole life. Penelope is like her in many ways. It's astounding how deep the similarities go between those two, and I don't just mean in how they look. But there was a reason Amos married Sarah, and now I understand why. The same qualities in Penelope appeal to me. Is there a genetic component to attraction?" he ended in a mocking tone.

"Nein, I don't believe there is," replied the bishop with seriousness. "All marriages are based on three principles—faith, finances and family. Among the Amish, attitudes toward faith and family are always the same, and presumably finances as well since we all ascribe to live according to biblical values toward money."

"That is a sticking point," admitted Simon. "She says she has some debt and is eager to pay it off."

"The fact that she's not actively accruing more debt means the situation is likely to have been a one-off, then," said the bishop. "But she was raised *Englisch.* Her position on faith and family may be vastly different than yours."

"Ja," agreed Lois. "Those are things you must discuss in advance and in detail. That's why I feel this interest in her may be little more than a crush rather than the deep-seated love that a marriage requires. It's too soon

to know where her path may lay. I'm worried you may be pinning hopes where hope doesn't exist."

"I urge caution," the bishop agreed. "Penelope has a lot to pull her toward our church, but right now she's wrestling with some big spiritual things and hasn't given much thought toward what she would give up if she became Amish. And as an *Englischer*, she would be giving up a lot—probably more than she even realizes at this point. These things can't be rushed."

Simon met the older man's eyes. "I've waited twenty-eight years to find a wife, Bishop. I can wait a bit longer. But I can't shake the feeling she might be the one *Gott* has in mind for me. I've tried to talk myself out of it. Amos has already verbally smacked me upside the head a couple of times, and tried to talk sense into me. But why would *Gott* put her here if not for a deeper purpose? However," he added, "I have no intention of breaching my baptismal vows in pursuit of an *Englischer*, no matter how attractive I may find her."

"*Gut* to know," said Beiler with firmness. "You've always been a fine, upstanding man in our community, Simon. I'd hate for that to change."

"Me, too." Defeated, Simon drained his glass and stood up. "I suppose I can't do anything more at the moment except leave things in *Gott*'s hands. I will school myself for patience, Bishop, and pray that Penelope comes to us of her own free will. If not…well, maybe the Amish should develop a system for mail-order brides."

The bishop chuckled. "It's been done a few times in the past, but it's just as chancy for long-term happiness as falling for an *Englischer*. I don't recommend it."

"Then I may as well prepare myself to stay single."

He couldn't help the harsh note that crept into his voice. "Most Amish women of marriageable age don't want a crusty bachelor approaching thirty. Maybe I can find a young widow."

"Simon, don't become bitter," advised Lois. "The future isn't clear to any of us, and bitterness solves nothing. Pray on it, as will we. Meanwhile, recognize that Penelope's faith is still in its infancy. It's not fair to expect her to think or behave as someone more mature in their beliefs. Be patient with her and let her grow."

"Ja, ja." Simon passed a hand over his face. *"Es tut mir leid.* I'm sorry. I don't mean to take anything out on you. I'm just…disappointed, I guess, that there isn't a quick or easy solution to this issue."

"Quick and easy is not the Amish way," noted Lois with an encouraging smile. "But often the trials and tribulations we experience create the strongest bonds. Remember what the Bible says about how going through the crucible of refinement creates the purest gold. We'll keep you in prayer, Simon."

"Danke." Nodding to both, he donned his hat and left the Beilers' home.

Nothing had been solved. Simon clenched his fists in frustration. He was still left dangling, wanting a woman he could not have and kicking himself for having admitted as much to her.

Chapter Fourteen

Penelope sensed Simon's withdrawal right away, and she was puzzled and hurt by it. What had happened that he was no longer the warm and interested man who had caught her attention? Was the painting she had given him offensive? He seemed to like it. Or was their mutual attraction so dangerous that he could no longer even look her in the eye?

Though she was here on business, the B&B's appeal—for her—was not so much its rural nature or off-grid charm. Rather, it had to do with the man who ran it. She enjoyed his company, his conversation and his wisdom.

Seeking wisdom of her own, she decided to walk over and see her sister. She wasn't sure if Sarah could offer any insight, but she trusted her twin's intuition. Besides, she needed someone to talk to.

Slipping out of the house the next morning, Penelope walked toward Sarah's home. The day promised to be warm. Late summer was upon the region, and while Montana lacked the humidity she was used to in Pennsylvania and Massachusetts, she knew she could expect some hot days ahead.

Ahead. Penelope stopped suddenly and realized "ahead"

was unlikely to happen here. Something told her the QuirkyB&B people were losing patience with her.

She sighed and started walking again. Life here could be very simple, she suspected. Instead, somehow, she had brought endless complications with her.

That's why she sought Sarah's input. Her sister seemed to lead a life of enviable simplicity, one that Penelope longed for more and more.

She found Sarah in the kitchen kneading bread. "*Komm* in!" her sister called in response to her knock. "*Guten tag*, Penelope."

"*Guten tag.* Bread?"

"*Ja.*" Sarah had a smudge of flour on her nose that made her look adorable. She had started wearing more loose-fitting clothing as her pregnancy advanced.

"Where are the children?" Penelope glanced around but saw no indication of the young ones.

"Amos has Paul with him on a trip to town, and Eleanor is napping. Would you like some tea?"

"Yes, please. No, don't stop, I'll make it." Penelope was familiar enough with her sister's kitchen by now to brew a cup for herself.

When the beverage was steeping, Penelope seated herself at the table and watched Sarah's capable hands knead the bread dough. "Sarah, can I ask you something?"

"*Ja*, sure." Sarah's glance sharpened. "Anything wrong?"

"Maybe. I'm not sure." She sighed and related the issue of Simon's sudden coldness. "I don't know what changed him," she concluded. "I thought we were becoming friends, but suddenly it's like I'm just a guest again. I mean, that's what I *am*, but up until this point it's not how he'd been treating me. If any of this makes sense," she added on a note of frustration.

"Penelope…" Sarah looked troubled. "If I may ask, why does Simon's withdrawal bother you so much?"

"Well…" Penelope looked at the table and didn't know what to say.

"That's what I thought." Her sister sighed. "I don't know if you're aware of the serious repercussions if a baptized Amish man were to fall in love with an *Englisch* woman. *Liebling*, Simon may have pulled back for the very reasons you mention. He might be looking at you more as a friend than as a guest. And as you're an *Englischer*, he can't risk it going any further."

"Yes, he said as much. He said it's because I'm not Amish."

"*Ja*, exactly so. He's baptized, Penelope, and that's a serious vow. As serious as wedding vows."

"Then we seem to have gotten ourselves into a pickle." Penelope dipped her tea bag up and down in hot water as she watched Sarah knead the dough. "We both feel an attraction, and apparently there's nothing that can be done about it. But now that he's pulled away, I realize how much I miss him."

"Do you want some advice, *meine schwester*?"

"Yes, of course. That's why I came over."

"You aren't going to like what I have to say, and it's this. Don't toy with his affections. He's pulled away for a reason. He knows the stakes involved and isn't willing to risk it."

"Because of shunning, you mean?"

"*Ja*, shunning. It's just a word, but it's a word that can't even begin to describe the all-encompassing horror of what would happen if he pursued his interest in you. He would lose everything."

Penelope gave a humorless bark of laughter. "Ironically, what would solve this is if I became Amish."

"*Liebling*, you weren't raised Amish. The likelihood of converting is low."

"I know." She stared at her tea. "But it's weird. Maybe it's because of you, but I want to stay here and get further involved in the community. The bishop and I had a conversation about the issue of being called. He said if God is calling me, I should *listen*. But I guess the problem is, I don't know how. How can I hear God's voice? How do I know it's Him rather than fear or anxiety or longing or any other emotion? I've even tried praying about it, but I don't know if He hears my prayers."

"*Gott* always hears our prayers," replied Sarah with confidence. "As for hearing His voice, maybe it just takes some practice, but eventually you'll be able to distinguish it from other emotions. It takes time, Penelope."

"And time is something I don't have." Penelope wrapped her hands around the tea mug and stared at the beverage.

"Why?" asked Sarah, pushing vigorously on the dough. "You're a traveling artist. Why not stay longer and see if you can discern *Gott*'s voice? You're welcome to move in with us and stay as long as you like. I enjoy having you close. I've even… Well, to confess, I've already set up the spare bedroom upstairs for you. Just in case. Staying with us would save you the cost of the B&B, and it would more fully immerse you in an Amish home to see if this is a lifestyle you could handle."

Penelope smiled at her mirror image. "You make it sound so simple."

"It's *supposed* to be simple," observed Sarah. "A simple life is nothing more than making *gut* choices."

Penelope startled. "Making good choices…" she echoed. "Is that it?"

"What else could it be? If you make the choice to rob a bank, your life becomes very complicated. But if you make the choice to worship *Gott* and behave in ways that are pleasing to Him, it becomes much simpler."

Penelope smiled at the pure wisdom of those words. "Seeking a simple life is a huge trend in society right now, but I think the Amish found the secret long ago," she said. "That's why everyone looks at you and envies your 'simple' lives. They just don't want to do what it takes to emulate that simplicity, which is doubtless why Amish converts don't last. Am I right?"

"*Ja*, I think you are." Sarah gave the bread dough a final pummeling, then shaped it into a ball, dropped the dough into a greased bowl, covered it with a towel and put the dough in a sunny patch by the window. "I know it would be less work—less physical work—if I went into the *Englisch* world, a place where I could just go buy bread instead of making it. But what would I find in its place? It seems to me *Englisch* society is very complicated, very hustle and bustle with no time to listen to *Gott*."

"Maybe that's why I've been able to hear God for the first time since coming here," said Penelope slowly. "And I had to leave society behind to do it."

"No doubt," agreed Sarah. She washed her hands and made her own cup of tea, then sat opposite Penelope. "If you want my honest opinion, I think we're more alike than just physical similarities. I think you have a longing to know *Gott*, just as I know Him. I just got an earlier start than you, that's all."

"Since we're being truthful," said Penelope with a wry smile, "then this is the point where I admit I've envied you since the first time I met you. You have no doubts or questions about your life. You have a solid standing in the community, the respect of everyone in your church, the love of a good man, and two and a half wonderful children."

"*Ja*, I'm blessed beyond measure." Sarah's eyes took on a misty glow, then her gaze sharpened. "But none of that is beyond you, either. It's something to think about. You also may want to talk to the bishop about these conflicted feelings. He's a *gut* man, and a wise one."

"Yes, I noticed that…"

A baby's cry came from another room. "Eleanor is awake," said Sarah, rising to her feet.

"And I should get going." Penelope also rose to her feet. "Thank you for the tea and the wisdom, Sarah."

Sarah leaned over and bestowed a hug. "I'm so glad you're here," she said. "*Bitte*, think about the offer to move in with us. Meanwhile, you might consider another talk with the bishop about becoming Amish, if you're seriously thinking about it."

"I will." Penelope returned the hug, placed her tea mug in the sink and left her sister's house.

It was a lot to think about.

Simon worked in the suite where the Holmes family was staying, making beds and freshening everything up with clean towels. He smiled at the scattering of toys from the little girls. He wondered if he would ever have toys scattered around from his own children…

He headed down the hall, arms full of soiled towels, when he was stopped by the sound of Penelope's voice—and the voice of another man. Evidently she was talking to someone on speakerphone, something he knew she sometimes did while painting.

He paused, conflicted. He desperately wanted to eavesdrop, but knew it was unethical to listen in on a private conversation. He had already done that once, and it left him in a mess. Yet if he could get any clarity about this mystery job and why she was here…

"Why haven't you answered my emails?" growled a surly voice.

"You knew this place was off-grid," replied Penelope. "And you knew I couldn't text. I have to go all the way into town to get emails."

"Sounds to me like you're avoiding any communication," countered the man, with the attitude of someone who woke up on the wrong side of the bed. "What's the situation with the franchise?"

Simon heard Penelope sigh. "It hasn't been easy," she said. "Nothing I've done has convinced the owner that franchising is worthwhile. He's independent-minded and determined to make it on his own."

Franchising, thought Simon. *So that's why she's here…*

"Then sweeten the deal," snapped the man. "Tell him what the advantages are…"

"I've worked in marketing, Frank," said Penelope. Simon heard anger in her voice. "I know all about sweetening deals and pushing advantages. I also know there's a subset of people who can't be swayed by financial arguments, and that's the situation I'm facing here. If he's not motivated by money, what other incentive can I offer?"

"Then it's time to play hardball," growled Frank. "You'll need to plant some poor reviews online. When's the last time you saw a cockroach in your room or found a hair in your food? You can start with those."

"You're talking nonsense," Penelope snapped. "I've never seen a cockroach here or found a hair in my food."

"Of course you have. And you're going to write reviews about those sad experiences, under a variety of different names and different accounts, and scare people off from staying at his place. Then, when it seems like he has no choice but to close the business, we'll swoop in and save the day by offering to franchise. Remember that nice hefty commission, Penelope."

Simon gripped his burden of towels with fury. He couldn't listen anymore and crept away from the hall where he had overheard the entire conversation. His heart pounded, and he alternated between despair and fury.

Penelope wasn't who she said she was. She wasn't an artist; she was an undercover scout for this corporate B&B company. Her job here wasn't to paint, though she undoubtedly was doing just that. Her job here was to bully him into becoming franchised by this company, allegedly for his own good.

He scowled. Whatever this company was, he didn't take seriously the threat of poor reviews or whatever they talked about. Most of his business came through word of mouth anyway and wasn't likely to be affected by whatever online shenanigans they tried to pull on him.

No, it was the sense of betrayal by Penelope herself. Was he mad to fall in love with her—an *Englischer* no less—when he knew nothing about her background or financial situation or…or anything?

"Schtupid," he muttered to himself. He stomped through the lobby, through the dining hall, through his still-disheveled private quarters and emerged from the house into the garden. There he found himself a crate to sit on near the chicken coop. Watching the chickens was, to him, a soothing pastime.

But this time his chaotic thoughts refused to be pacified. He found himself angrier at himself than he was at Penelope—angry for falling for someone so wildly ineligible.

How many hints had she given over her stay that she wasn't who she said she was? He remembered—clearly—the first time he had inquired about her art. She had acted trapped and cornered. While it was clear she was a talented artist, it was just as clear it wasn't how she earned her living. So much for being the roaming artist she claimed to be.

How could he look her in the eye anymore? How could he continue to treat her with the respect a paying guest normally commanded? At his moment, he hardly wanted to see her at all.

And yet, as the professional hotelier he claimed he was, he could hardly refuse her business. She was paying for her stay here…

He made a silent promise to go into town and talk to his *Englisch* friend who had built the website for him, to ask his friend to monitor for the things Penelope had been instructed to do—write bad reviews and post them online. Simon wasn't sure how that worked, so he hoped his *Englisch* friend did.

"Simon?"

He jerked his head up. Penelope approached him through the garden, a blend of defiance and defeat on her face.

"What?"

"Simon, there's something I need to tell you…"

"Don't bother," he said harshly. He jumped to his feet so quickly that the crate upended behind him, startling some of the chickens, which squawked and flapped to the far side of the enclosure. "I overheard your conversation."

"Y-you overheard?" she stammered. "What did you overhear?"

"The conversation you just had with the man about franchising my B&B."

"Oh." She dropped her gaze to the gravel under her feet. "That's what I wanted to talk to you about."

"What is there to talk about?" he snapped. "You've deceived me from the beginning. Now you've been instructed to falsify online reviews about my business. Do I have that right?"

"Y-yes," she said, and her eyes were suddenly bright with unshed tears. He refused to be moved. "But there's more to it than that. Please, Simon, I want you to hear what I have to say."

"Frankly, Penelope, I'm far too angry right now to listen." He moved toward the garden gate. "I have an errand in town. I could put it off, but right now I need space to think. Excuse me." Rudely he elbowed past her and headed for the house.

He opted to walk to town in an effort to blow off steam. It took him less than an hour to traverse the three-mile distance, and he was still frosted by the time he arrived at his friend's office.

"Hello, Greg," he greeted the nerdy-looking young man sitting behind a desk.

"Simon!" Greg jumped up and pumped Simon's hand. "Didn't expect to see you today!"

"*Ja*, well, I have a pressing concern I wanted to bring to your attention."

"Sure. What's up?"

Simon explained about the possibility of false reviews being posted concerning his B&B. "I don't have any idea how to find such things, much less indicate they're incorrect," he concluded. "I was hoping you could do some routine monitoring on my website and make any corrections, then bill me monthly for your time."

"The reviews wouldn't be on your website," said Greg thoughtfully. He sat down at his desk and typed rapidly. "See? Nothing can be added or changed except by admin, which is me. I'm guessing the reviews would get posted on various public forums for trip advice and B&B ratings websites. Not much I can do about those, except to post a rebuttal if I see one."

"So if something is posted on one of these public forums, it can't be removed?" Simon frowned. "That seems like it would be subject to a lot of abuse by people who want to cause trouble."

"Yes, it's often abused like that. Lots of people in this world have nothing better to do than cause trouble."

Greg rubbed his chin. "But I'll do as you ask and keep my eyes peeled for anything that crops up regarding your specific B&B."

"*Ja, danke.* Thank you," said Simon. "Keep track of your hours and bill me for whatever you do."

"It shouldn't be much," replied Greg. "I can automate a lot of it. Don't let it worry you, Simon," he added. "Frankly it sounds like a bunch of tough talk without much to back it up."

"I hope you're right," Simon replied. "Thank you, Greg."

He plopped his hat back on his head and started on the long road back toward his house. He was still steamed. Not only was Penelope costing him extra money, but he was being forced to monitor a situation that had no basis in fact. He had never given any thought to what kind of information about his B&B was posted online outside of his own website, and it chilled him to think all his hard work could be sabotaged simply because Penelope was looking for some way to pay off her debt.

He hated the sense of betrayal that plagued him.

Chapter Fifteen

Penelope watched Simon stalk away and her heart sank. Of all the stupid times to put someone on speakerphone, why this time?

She sank down on the crate Simon had vacated and stared blindly at the chickens scratching and clucking in their yard. What should she do? How could she convince him her intentions were honorable?

The fact of the matter was, her intentions were *not* honorable. Her purpose here was to convince Simon to franchise, and the fact that she had lost heart in the attempt didn't change why she had come here to begin with. Her boss's smarmy tactics to sabotage the business were just part of the continuum of ugly things she was supposed to do for this company.

During their conversation, Frank had picked up on her internal conflict with a surety born of experience. "All scouts feel this way with their first assignment," he had said in a more convincing voice. "It gets easier, Penelope, truly it does."

"What gets easier?" she said wearily. "Fraud and deceit?"

"But you forget, that B&B will benefit greatly by being franchised. What does it matter how it happens?

The owner will be listed on one of the most user-friendly booking sites available. Undoubtedly he'll be *swamped* with business. The contrast between what he's experiencing now and what he can experience as a QuirkyB&B member will be night and day. From what you've said, it sounds like this guy has a good head on his shoulders. As a businessman, he'll appreciate the benefits we offer…"

Frank had droned on and on, using the same persuasive tactics Penelope had learned during her training session…except this time she could see through the arguments to the flawed logic behind them. How could she have been so blind as to not see through the baloney?

"I'll try my best, Frank," she said at last.

"First assignments are always tough, honey," Frank had said. "Don't let it get you down. After a few times, you'll wonder why you ever doubted your ability to get the job done."

Penelope winced at his use of the endearment *honey*.

"I don't know if this will ever get easier," she warned him. "But if I can't persuade Mr. Troyer to agree to franchise, maybe you should just find me my next assignment."

"If there is one," Frank concluded ominously. "And remember, you're staying at that B&B on your own dime until we reimburse you from our corporate account. If you fail to accomplish this assignment, not only will you forfeit your commission, but you'll be paying for your room yourself."

"Do you mean to tell me," said Penelope in a horrified voice, "that you're refusing to cover my expenses if I fail to achieve a franchise? That was never in my contract."

"So sue me," Frank said nastily. "On paper, you're

simply taking an extended vacation to practice painting. Why should we pay for that?"

"Because you told me from the beginning that my expenses on the road would be covered!" she shouted.

"Don't lose your temper with me, kiddo," sneered Frank in a condescending tone. "You don't get ahead in this business by being nice. Goodbye."

The phone connection had clicked off. Penelope had stared at it, unable to believe the mess she was in.

She couldn't do it. She couldn't lie about Simon's business, or leave false reviews under fake accounts, or do anything that might sabotage what she recognized was a superb business.

But quitting this job now meant more than simply forfeiting her commission. It would also mean an extra few thousand dollars on her credit card—her personal credit card—from her extended stay here at Simon's B&B.

Frank's threats were legitimate. As she sat in the garden after Simon's angry departure, problem piled upon problem until she was frozen in fear and uncertainty.

Suddenly she had a vision of what Sarah might say if she knew if this circumstances. "Pray," she had suggested one time.

So Penelope tried it. Tentatively, timidly, she looked upward and whispered, "Guide me, Lord. What do I do?"

Suddenly, urgently, she had a sense she should talk to the bishop. But this time, she would be completely truthful.

She jumped up from the crate, left the garden and started walking down the gravel road toward the bishop's house, hoping he was home.

During the walk, she wondered how she was going

to broach the various subjects on her mind. There was so much ricocheting around her brain that she almost didn't know where to start. Foremost, of course, was the hurt she had inflicted on Simon and the remorse she felt at betraying him. But there was more.

The Beilers' little farm looked fruitful and inviting as she approached it. Penelope climbed the porch steps and knocked on the screen door, then waited for a response, her heart beating fast.

To her relief, she saw Lois Beiler approach. *"Guten tag!"* she greeted, opening the screen. Then her smile dropped and her eyes widened. "You look troubled, child."

At the unexpected sympathy, Penelope blinked back sudden tears. "I am," she confirmed. She gave an inelegant sniff. "I'm sorry to drop by unexpectedly, but is your husband home? I could use a little advice right now."

"He's in his study. Why don't you have a seat and I'll let him know you're here?"

"You know, Mrs. Beiler, I wonder if I shouldn't have you sit in on my discussion with the bishop. It might be useful to have your perspective."

"Ja sure." Lois stood back and motioned for Penelope to enter the house. "And I have some iced tea in the icebox. I'll fetch some."

Penelope sank down in one of the Beilers' comfortable rocking chairs. She heard Lois speak quietly in German to her husband before retreating to the kitchen to prepare beverages.

Samuel Beiler came into the living room. *"Guten tag,* Penelope," he greeted, scanning her face. "My wife tells me you're troubled."

"Yes," she said. She clasped her hands in her lap. "I

hope you have time to discuss some things? I have a lot on my plate."

"And I have a lot of tea on my tray," quipped Lois, entering the living room with a tray of drinks. She passed them around, then sank into a chair nearby while the bishop folded himself into what was clearly his favorite seat.

In the brief and expectant silence, Penelope sipped her tea for something to do. "I almost don't know where to start," she confessed. "Maybe brute honesty is the best course of action."

In fact, if she had any sort of future in this community at all, she realized with sudden clarity, the church leader needed to be fully aware of her background.

"Let me back up to a few months ago," she began. "As you may or may not know, I used to work at a marketing and advertising firm in Boston. I got laid off at about the same time my apartment rent skyrocketed. I was searching for a job, but having a hard time finding anything. I was competing in a limited job market against a bunch of people who were better qualified and more educated than I am. My parents always taught me to avoid debt, but I had no choice but to pay for my rent two months in a row on my credit card. And rent in Boston is very expensive," she added.

Lois Beiler winced. "So you haven't been able to pay it off?"

"No. And when I landed another job, one of the reasons I took it was because I would be living on the road and wouldn't have to worry about rent. But now I have something else to worry about."

"But I thought you were an artist…" began the bishop in some bewilderment.

"This takes some explaining," sighed Penelope. She told the older couple everything—her newly found position as a scout, her expected commission that would be enough to pay off her debt, the high-pressure tactics she was instructed to use on Simon, the subterfuge that she was nothing more than a traveling artist as a front for her extended stay.

"It all came crashing down when Simon introduced me to Sarah," she admitted. "Suddenly this assignment was no longer an impersonal job. Instead, I was being asked to take advantage of a relative, as it were. And... and I couldn't do it. I couldn't do it because of Sarah, and I... I couldn't do it to Simon."

"Well, I admire you for that..." began Samuel Beiler.

"But it gets worse," said Penelope. She fished a handkerchief out of her pocket and mopped eyes that were suspiciously moist. "I had an irate call from my boss a little while ago. Not only was he annoyed because I couldn't convince Simon to franchise his business, but then he wanted me to leave false reviews as a method of sabotaging Simon. He told me the company wouldn't pay my expenses if I didn't. This would mean that in addition to my apartment rent, I'm responsible for my living expenses since arriving here in Pierce. Instead of getting out of debt, I'm deeper in debt than ever before, unless I agree to sabotage Simon's business. Then to make it even worse, Simon overheard part of the phone call in which this was explained, and he's understandably furious. It just seems like door after door is slamming shut on me."

"Oh, *liebling*..." Lois Beiler patted Penelope's knee. "There's an old expression: when *Gott* closes a door,

He opens a window. You just haven't found your window yet."

Penelope sniffed and blew her nose. "I don't know what to do," she admitted. "More and more, I find I want to stay here. Stay near Sarah, of course, but also…also…"

"Stay near Simon?" suggested Lois.

"Yes." The tears came then, and she sobbed in frustration. "I know exactly why it's not possible to have a future with him. He knows it, too. So it seems I'm stuck between a rock and a hard place, pulled in seven different directions and unable to see a way out for any of them." She buried her face in the handkerchief and tried to compose herself.

There was a moment's silence in the room.

"When you say you want to stay," began the bishop, "can you explain further?"

Penelope mopped her face and looked over at the church leader. "You told me once that Amish converts are rare," she said. "I've been reading some of the books Simon keeps in the lobby on Amish culture and beliefs. I have no hope you'd ever consider me as a candidate for conversion, so it seems hopeless to try and stay here."

"Hopeless?" said Lois in a quiet voice. "Why do you say that?"

"Because from what I gather, a romantic interest is not a strong enough reason to join the group," replied Penelope with as much dignity as she could muster. "The conversion must be faith-based."

"And you don't have enough faith?" the older woman persisted.

"I don't know," replied Penelope, suddenly unsure. She glanced at the bishop, who was listening intently.

"I told you once before that this void inside me seems less empty since I've started attending the church services and even reading the Bible in my room. But those are baby steps. You're all so mature in your faith, and I'm an amateur. That's why I would never presume to be considered."

To her surprise, the bishop gave a quiet chuckle. "You'd be surprised how many requests I've gotten over the years from people convinced they'd make the perfect Amish member," he said. "Most of them are what I call 'simple-life seekers' who see only the quaint and superficial aspects of our lifestyle. What they can't or won't admit is how our faith underpins everything we do—how we live, how we dress, everything about us. But you," he added thoughtfully, "are a bit different."

Penelope felt a thin shaft of hope go through her. "Different?" she repeated. "Different how?"

"I won't say genetics have anything to do with it, but the fact remains you were born of an Amish mother and have an Amish twin. Those are powerful tugs, and while I won't go so far as to imply they have a spiritual basis, I won't deny there might be a pull for you. You've certainly made a lot of effort to participate in the community, including practicing the language. I wonder if this is all part of the call you mentioned earlier?"

"But that puts me back at square one," she said with a trace of impatience. "How do I know if a call is genuine, or just the result of a lot of wishful thinking?"

"It takes time," advised the bishop. "Time to discern between the two. Wishful thinking loses its luster after a while. A true calling doesn't."

"So where do I go from here?" she demanded.

The bishop leaned back in his chair. "Let me ask you something," he said. "If you didn't have this debt hanging over your head, what would you do?"

"Quit my job," she replied promptly. "Mend fences with Simon. Move in with Sarah—she and Amos have already said I could stay with them. Maybe get a job locally to work off what I owe. And paint. I've enjoyed being able to paint."

"Those are good, solid plans," the older man replied. "What's preventing you from following through right now?"

Penelope stared at the floor. Could she do it? Could she just…quit? Mend fences with Simon?

"You make it sound so easy," she murmured after a while.

"Sometimes we tend to make things more complicated than they have to be," replied the bishop. "But it sounds to me like you know exactly what you want. As for converting and becoming Amish—well, that's a bridge to cross later. However, one thing is certain—you won't know whether you have a true calling to convert unless you spend enough time with us to discern whether it's genuine or not."

"I guess I could find a job locally," she ventured. She managed a rusty chuckle. "Ironically, I have the skills to help Simon," she remarked. "The very weaknesses that brought his B&B to the attention of the company I work for—namely, poor marketing and minimal advertising—are my strengths. I have a lot of experience with those. Together we could make a formidable team to make his B&B a success. But now I suspect he just wants me to go away, and I can't blame him."

"Simon can be stubborn," conceded the church leader. "He is determined to prove to his father that he can make the business a success on his own terms, for example. If you were to offer your help, I think that might go a long way toward making up for the circumstances which brought you out here."

"Brought me out here…" she repeated. She offered the couple a tremulous smile. "Simon and Sarah both had suggested that the reason I ended up here, of all places in the nation, where my twin sister would be, was the hand of God. Maybe they were right, and I'm supposed to stay."

"It's certainly something to think about," said the bishop. "Now, another question. How do your parents feel about the issue? I assume you've been in communication with them."

At the mention of the people who raised her, Penelope felt a flush of love go through her. "They were both dismayed and thrilled to learn I have a twin," she said. "Dismayed because they never knew and certainly would not have hesitated to raise us both. And thrilled that Sarah and I found each other. They're fully supportive of the idea of staying here, and may come out to visit if I do."

"That's *gut*, then. I would not have wanted you to do anything to cause bad blood between you and them."

"They would like to meet Sarah," she said. "And Sarah received a letter from her own parents that they'd like to meet me. It seems I have vastly more family connections than I ever knew about."

"A blessing from *Gott*," observed Lois Beiler.

"Yes."

"So it seems to me you have your path laid before

you," advised the bishop. "You can even make a list if you want. Quit your job, mend fences with Simon, move in with Sarah and Amos, and get a local job to pay down your debt. It's all very simple. After that, we'll see where things go."

Penelope gave a shaky laugh. *"Danke,"* she replied. "But I think I'll reverse the first two items. I'll mend fences with Simon before anything else."

"That would be wise," agreed Lois. Her eyes twinkled. "Doing that will make the other things easier."

The skies grew cloudy as Simon stalked back to the B&B in a foul mood. Despite his anger at Penelope, he had guests to attend to, both the Holmes family and Leonard Baskin. He didn't want to risk a real-life bad review simply because he was angry at the possibility of fake ones being posted online.

It just seemed like the world around him was imploding, and it all was because of Penelope. At this point he just wanted her gone. That way he could mourn her departure in private and then get on with his life.

He entered his home and made his way toward the kitchen, where he commenced making dinner. He yanked ingredients together and began assembling a chicken-and-dumpling casserole.

He still had a lot to prove to his father about the B&B's success. Without the distraction of that beautiful woman in the upstairs room, maybe he could do more toward—

"There you are."

He looked up to see her walking across the dining room toward the kitchen's service window.

"Go away," he said crossly. "I don't want to talk to you."

"Yes, you do," she contradicted. Uninvited, she walked around the wall and entered the kitchen. "Because you'll want to hear about the discussion I just had with Bishop Beiler."

"The bishop?" he parroted. "You went to see the bishop?"

"Yes. Lois Beiler was there, too. I had a lot of things to resolve, and wanted their advice."

"Did you tell them about this wonderful job of yours?" he asked sarcastically.

"As a matter of fact, I did. My thought was if I'm going to have a future in this community, then I needed to lay everything in front of them."

Despite his resentment, Simon felt a shaft of hope slice through him. "A future in this community," he repeated. "What do you mean?"

She washed her hands and started dicing the celery on the cutting board. "You've been clueless about what's happening on my end because until you overheard that phone call, you had no idea what I've been battling. Let me begin at the beginning."

She chopped the celery with what seemed like unnecessary vigor while she related a tale of woe about a job layoff and rent increases. "I was getting desperate," she said, her eyes on the knife in her hand. "This offer came up from a company called QuirkyB&B, which specializes in finding what their name implies—funky or unusual bed-and-breakfast businesses around the country—and franchising them under the Quirky umbrella. Essentially they would require certain uniform standards and provide increased marketing opportunities in exchange for a share of the profits."

"But I don't understand," said Simon in some bewilderment. "I'm a brand-new start-up business in an obscure little town in the back end of Montana. How did a business like this even know about me?"

"Among much else, they scour chambers of commerce of small towns all across the country, looking for just such businesses. Ironically, your poor online presence is what brought you to their attention. They figured you would be vulnerable and so eager for financial assistance that you'd be a shoo-in to franchise."

"So you took the job."

"Yes. They were 'always hiring,' they told me during the interview, and assured me my skills were valuable. Now I know why they're 'always hiring.' Once their scouts get pushed from high-pressure tactics into the realm of shady and unethical, a lot of them quit."

"So you're not an artist, then."

She gave him a sad smile. "Yes and no. Obviously I can paint, but I've never sold a painting. I've always given them away to friends and family. But QuirkyB&B said it was best if scouts could have a cover, an excuse for why they had a prolonged stay at any location, and my art was that excuse."

"In other words," he said grimly, "your presence here has been based on lies since the very beginning."

She met his eyes. "Yes."

"And you expect me to be happy about that?"

"Of course not! But this whole thing was coming to a head anyway. The phone call you overheard was just the latest in a series of increasingly irritated communications with my boss. Meanwhile, of course, this credit card bill has been hanging over my head and I had no hopes of paying it off except through the commission I was going to earn by convincing you to franchise. It started to feel like a type of blood money," she added. "That's why I went to talk to the bishop."

"And what did the bishop say?"

"He said I have four tasks to accomplish." She finished dicing the celery and put the knife down. "Number one was to mend fences with you, and number two was to quit my job. He suggested I quit my job first and mend fences second, but I think reversing that is more important."

"Quit your job…"

"Yes." She met his eyes, and he saw pleading in their dark depths. "I can't sabotage your business. But I *can* help you with it. I have experience with marketing and advertising. I have a lot to make up to you, and I thought that might be a good place to start."

Simon's knotted-up midsection started to unravel. "You said four tasks. What are the other two?"

"Move in with Sarah—who's already invited me, by the way—and lastly get a local job so I can pay down my debt. This would also serve to keep me in the community to see if…if…" Her voice trailed off.

"To see if what?" he asked gently.

"To see if I want to convert and become Amish," she admitted.

A golden shaft of sunlight pierced the thickening clouds and lit up the kitchen from the western window. Simon stared into her dark eyes, and he felt a trembling hope start deep inside.

"Are you serious?" he croaked.

She nodded. "I've been trying to decide if the feeling inside me to stay here is wishful thinking or a true calling. The bishop said time will tell, and that means staying here longer than I intended, and that means quitting my job." Her face crumpled. "Oh, Simon, I never meant to deceive you. I was just so desperate to pay off my credit card that I didn't think how unethical this company was, or how much it would hurt you to try and convince you to be franchised."

He forgave her on the spot. He so desperately wanted her to stay and become part of the church that he would have been willing to forgive a lot more.

"In the end, no harm was done," he said. "And much *gut* came of it. It sounds like the only thorny thing left on your plate is to pay off your debt, and a local job will take care of that. It might take a while, but it's doable."

She sniffed, then gave him a brilliant smile. "It means moving out," she warned. "I can't afford to stay here if I'm going to focus on paying down the credit card. But I'm serious about my offer to help with marketing and advertising. Let's see if between us we can't fill up every room in this house."

He tipped back his head and laughed. From bleak to golden, his world had changed in the space of ten minutes. *"Danke, Gott,"* he choked. Then he met her eyes. "And if you decide to become baptized, will you let me court you?"

"Of course." Her eyes were bright with unshed tears. "I'm counting on it."

He snaked his hands around her waist and drew her close. "It could be a long procedure," he warned. "I'm guessing two or more years before the bishop will agree to baptize you."

"I hope I'm worth the wait," she replied. She looped her hands around his neck and pressed her forehead to his. "I feel a thousand pounds lighter at the thought of quitting my job, and a wait of two years will give me the time to find a job and pay off my credit card."

The kiss that followed was unfortunately interrupted by the entrance of Mr. Baskin, the middle-aged guest. Simon and Penelope sprang apart, and Simon tried to pretend he had not just experienced an earth-shattering embrace.

"Good afternoon," Baskin said, approaching the kitchen's service window. He jerked a thumb over his shoulder. "That painting in the lobby area above the bookcase—was that there this morning?"

"Ja," replied Simon. He flashed a lightning glance at Penelope and saw laughter dancing in her eyes. "But it's brand-new. I just hung it yesterday."

"I can't imagine how I didn't notice it earlier, then. Was it painted by someone local?"

"Ja. Very local, in fact."

"Well, I'd be interested in meeting the artist."

"Why?" piped up Penelope.

"Because I own a company that makes, among other things, jigsaw puzzles. There's a certain quality of artwork that makes for excellent puzzles, and I'm always on the lookout for new artists who can contribute toward our repertoire. Rural themes are very popular. Is there a way to contact the artist?"

Simon turned toward Penelope and saw utter shock on

her face. She opened and closed her mouth a few times, but no sound came out.

"I'm the artist," she finally croaked. "I gave the painting to Simon yesterday morning as a gift."

"Well, I'm impressed." Baskin reached into his back pocket and extracted a wallet, from which he withdrew a business card. He handed it to Penelope. "Where do you sell your art?"

"I don't." She took the card and glanced at it. "I've never sold a piece. I've only given them away to friends."

"You said your name was Penelope, right?"

"Yes, Penelope Moore."

He smiled. "Then I have a proposal that might interest you, Ms. Moore. Do you have other artwork I could look at?"

"Upstairs." She blinked hard, as if fighting tears. "I have a number of finished pieces upstairs in my room, with a couple more incomplete ones, as well as a sketchbook of future ideas."

"Have you ever thought about becoming a puzzle artist?"

"Mr. Baskin, I've never even *heard* of a puzzle artist."

The quip broke the tension, and Simon chuckled.

Leonard Baskin's eyes crinkled with humor. "Amish-themed artwork is one of our most popular categories," he told her. He glanced at her clothing. "Are you Amish?"

"Not yet." She gave him a brilliant smile. "But I may be, shortly."

Epilogue

~❧~

Two years later...

"Two years. It's hard to believe I've been here two years already." Penelope pointed. "And look at them."

Her parents and Sarah's parents were seated at a table, in the center of which was a large vase filled with leafy celery stalks. The couples were deep in discussion and seemed to be getting along swimmingly.

"Your parents are delightful," said Simon.

"So are Sarah's. We're both so fortunate to have the parents we do." She snaked a hand around his waist. "And now I get to stay near Sarah forever."

"And me. Don't forget about me."

She grinned at his mocking-hurt tone. "Oh, you mean you're part of the deal, too? I'd forgotten."

He chuckled. "Don't forget, I was right all along. It *was* the hand of *Gott* that brought you out to the B&B two years ago. Think of everything that's happened since then! Meeting Sarah, becoming a full-time artist, getting baptized last week and getting married an hour ago. What a journey."

"And it all started by the seed God planted when He brought me here."

"Don't forget the best wedding present I could imagine—my father's blessing on what I've—what *we've*—accomplished with the B&B. He and *Mamm* are delighted to be staying in it while visiting here."

"The whole B&B is like a huge family reunion of people who never knew they were related," said Penelope. She started ticking off on her fingers. "Your parents, my parents, Sarah's parents, your middle brother and his wife…what a full house!"

"Not full enough yet." He tightened his grip around her waist. "Now that you have an art studio built against the north side of the house, and now that your debt is long since paid off, I'm already planning additional expansions as…necessary."

"And 'necessary' could be sooner than we think. We have a lot of catching up to do with Amos and Sarah."

He kissed the tip of her nose. "How does it feel to be Mrs. Troyer?"

Penelope grinned at him. "Ask me that tomorrow."

* * * * *

If you liked this story from Patrice Lewis,
check out her previous Love Inspired books:

The Amish Beekeeper's Dilemma
The Amish Midwife's Bargain
Their Road to Redemption

Available now from Love Inspired!

Dear Reader,

I grew up with three brothers. As the only girl in the family, I longed for a sister. One day when I was about seven years old, I changed my hairstyle and tried to convince my friends that I was my own twin. (Spoiler alert: it didn't work.)

Twins have always fascinated me, and even now I still have a bit of envy for those who grew up with a built-in best friend. This is why it was fun to explore what it must be like to suddenly discover that long-lost twin in my character Penelope.

I enjoy hearing from readers, so feel free to email me at patricelewis@protonmail.com.

Patrice